"What's causing ⬚⬚⬚ **"**

"I didn't realize my fa⬚⬚⬚"

Marie laughed. "Well, it looks like a thundercloud, and I can't figure out why. You monopolized the belle of the ball yesterday. You should be happy, happy, happy this morning."

He smiled slightly. "You always have been a nosy brat. I didn't sleep much last night, so don't pick at me this morning."

Marie was always a person who sensed when others were downhearted, but judging from the humor mirrored in her eyes, she didn't realize how the hours he'd spent in the presence of Dora, a New York socialite, had changed his life. Allen had always considered himself immune from attractive women, but he'd overestimated his willpower. After he'd helped Dora in the forest, he had supposed she'd returned to New York, and he doubted that he'd ever see her again. Then yesterday he'd gone to that dedication. His first glimpse of Dora had hit him like a bolt of lightning. During the time they'd spent together, she'd made it fairly evident that she intended to keep in touch with him.

IRENE BRAND

is a lifelong resident of West Virginia, where she lives with her husband, Rod. Irene's first inspirational romance was published in 1984, and since that time she has had multiple books published. She is the author of four nonfiction books, various devotional materials, and her writings have appeared in numerous historical, religious, and general magazines. Irene became a Christian at the age of eleven and continues to be actively involved in her local church. Before retiring in 1989 to devote full time to freelance writing, Irene taught for twenty-three years in secondary public schools. Many of her books have been inspired while traveling to forty-nine of the United States and twenty-four foreign countries.

Books by Irene Brand

HEARTSONG PRESENTS

A Life
Worth Living

Irene Brand

Heartsong Presents

To Mary Lynn Bechtle,
my longtime friend and faithful reader.

A note from the Author:

*I love to hear from my readers! You may correspond with
me by writing:*

**Irene Brand
Author Relations
P.O. Box 9048
Buffalo, NY 14240-9048**

ISBN-13: 978-0-373-48646-5

A LIFE WORTH LIVING

This edition issued by special arrangement with Barbour Publishing,
Inc., 1810 Barbour Drive, Uhrichsville, Ohio, U.S.A.

Chapter 1

Asheville, North Carolina, 1895

Dora Porter had hiked through some of the most beautiful scenery Europe had to offer, but never had she seen a more majestic sight than the one before her. The only child of Oliver Porter, one of the richest entrepreneurs in the world, she had traveled throughout Europe marveling at the ancient buildings in Greece and scaling some of the most picturesque mountains in Switzerland. She hadn't thought any scenery could equal what she'd appreciated in those countries. But today, as she leaned against a towering pine, gazing toward the Blue Ridge Mountains, she conceded that this vista surpassed anything she'd seen in foreign lands.

Taking a small guidebook from her pocket, she read that the term *Blue Ridge* was usually applied exclusively to the front range of the Appalachians. She was surprised to note that the Blue Ridge extended as far north as the mountains of Massachusetts and Vermont. Although English travelers as early as the seventeenth century had visited the area, a German physician, John Lederer, was believed to have been the first European to visit the northern Blue Ridge at Harper's Ferry as early as 1669. As she beheld the beauty of the scenery before her, Dora decided that she'd probably missed a lot by not seeing more of her own country. She'd seen about all she wanted to see in Europe, so perhaps she should make arrangements to go to California next summer.

She had been somewhat reluctant when her father had insisted that she join him on this trip to North Carolina. Usually her father had an ulterior motive when he invited her to accompany him somewhere, and she had to be constantly on guard that he didn't involve her in something that she didn't want to do. But she had visited the home of George Vanderbilt and his mother in New York, and Dora had accepted an invitation to visit them at Biltmore, their new home in the Appalachian Mountains. Although a world traveler, George had also traveled extensively in the United States. On his first visit to North Carolina, he had been impressed with the area around Asheville. With its dramatic topography, distant views, and mild physical climate, he decided that the area would be a suitable location for another home. When Dora had visited the Vanderbilt home in New York, she'd often heard her father and George discussing the estate he was establishing in North Carolina. She'd been surprised that George, a man who liked to be involved in the political affairs of New York, would be interested in spending so much time in what her father referred to as a "godforsaken region."

She was still a bit suspicious of her father's reason for coming. Her father never did anything that wouldn't contribute to his wealth and prestige. He had seen his share of beautiful architecture, and she was sure something more than a visit to the Vanderbilt's mountain home had prompted him to come to North Carolina. Did that motive involve her, too? Why else would he have insisted that she accompany him? Although the invitation had come from Mrs. Vanderbilt, Dora was wary about its origin. Surely her father didn't think she was romantically interested in George. Actually, Dora wasn't romantically interested in anyone.

She wasn't surprised, then, when her father finally told her that he was drawn to the area due to the possibilities for industrial expansion in the Asheville area, the only town of any size in that part of the state. Always on the lookout for new ways to prosper, he had accepted an invitation to the opening and dedication of the Biltmore mansion.

Considering all the places she'd seen, as well as the wealth she'd inherited, Dora couldn't understand why she was so dissatisfied with her life. For the past several months, she had been critical of her past. As one of New York City's most popular women, she should have been proud of her achievements. However, when she considered her life since she'd entered her teen years, everything she'd done had been centered on herself. Except for an occasional check to charitable organizations, and in retrospect she realized that they hadn't been very generous, what had she done for other people?

Glancing at the watch pinned to her jacket, Dora turned toward Biltmore. Tomorrow would be a full day when George Vanderbilt would welcome his friends and neighbors to tour the palatial mansion that had been under construction for several years. Since she didn't know anyone in the area except George and his mother, she anticipated a boring day. Turning for one more glimpse of the mountains, Dora stumbled and suddenly found herself on the ground with her left foot wedged between a rock and the trunk of a pine tree.

A sharp pain in her ankle indicated that she had an injury, and she wondered how she could extricate herself from such a predicament. Efforts to free her foot brought only discomfort and aggravation. When she'd toured the Alps and other European mountains, she'd always traveled with a companion, but she hadn't thought it would be necessary in these gentle mountains. Should she call for help or wait until someone at Biltmore came looking for her? She heard footsteps approaching, and a young man wearing a red cap, overalls, and a light jacket suddenly appeared at her side. He was of medium height, and his wide shoulders and rugged appearance spoke of strength and vitality. He had thick dark hair, a ready smile, and a fine pair of brown eyes.

Surprise spread across his face, and for a few moments he stared at her. Dropping to one knee, he said, "Do you need help, ma'am?" Then he laughed. "I suppose that was a foolish question. Let me start over. What can I do to help you?"

"I wasn't paying enough attention when I turned to take one last look at the mountains, and my foot is wedged below this tree root. If you'll help me stand, I can determine whether I can walk or not. This is an awkward position. I'm so embarrassed to have been so clumsy."

"If you've broken a bone, you probably shouldn't put any weight on the injury, so lean on me until you're sure you can walk." Slowly and tenderly, he carefully freed her foot, stood behind her, put his arms around her waist, and lifted. She staggered, and his arms tightened. "Oh," she cried when she put weight on her foot.

"Careful now," he cautioned. "Hold on to me. I won't let you fall."

For a fleeting moment, Dora considered how great it would be to have someone to lean on occasionally. Since childhood, her father had insisted, *"It's only the pushers who get ahead in this world. Don't expect help from anyone else. Make your own future."* At this point, Dora doubted the wisdom of those words. She welcomed this man's help as she leaned heavily against his strong chest. Her arm circled his waist, which didn't seem to have an ounce of fat. He was a brawny man, and since she had always had to be self-sufficient, it gave her a vast boost of spirit and courage to lean against a man who seemed as strong as the Rock of Gibraltar.

"If you'll tell me where you live," he said, "I'll take you there or bring your family to look after you."

"Let me lean on you for a moment, and I'll see if I can walk. I'm embarrassed for anyone to know I was so careless. I'm Dora Porter, and my home is in New York City, but I'm visiting at Biltmore. My father and Mr. Vanderbilt are business associates, and he invited us for the opening of their home. And you?"

"My name is Allen Bolden. I'm a carpenter by trade, and I've worked off and on for Mr. Vanderbilt since he came here. I did some of the work on the mansion, but mostly on the outbuildings. I've lived in the area for a few years, and Mr. Vanderbilt hired me to look through this forest and determine whether the timber should be harvested now or wait for another year or two. What can I do to further help you?"

Dora continued to lean on his strength. "I don't want to cause any extra work at Biltmore when all the servants are busy preparing for the big celebration tomorrow. If you'll help me, I'll try to walk back to the house."

She took a tentative step and then another. "I don't believe I've sprained my ankle, but sharp pains flash through my foot every time I move. Perhaps you can go to Biltmore and ask someone to bring a cart to haul me to the house, although I don't want to cause a disturbance there. It must be more than a mile, and I doubt I'd have the strength to go that far. I have the reputation of being an outdoors person, and I've been hiking off and on for several years over rough terrain without an accident, so I'm embarrassed for anyone to see me like this. You're probably familiar with the old adage, 'Pride goeth before destruction, and an haughty spirit before a fall.' I guess I'm too proud of my experience as a hiker to want anyone to know that I was clumsy enough to catch my foot in a tree root."

"I know exactly how you feel. I've been climbing these mountains for several years, and I'd be embarrassed if I experienced an accident like yours. I'm heading in that direction to report to Mr. Vanderbilt, so I'll be pleased to help you to the house. With my help, you won't have to worry about falling. You might be able to sneak into the mansion without anyone knowing."

She hesitated. "I'd prefer that, if you're sure it isn't too much trouble."

"No trouble. I need to report my findings to Mr. Vanderbilt."

Her rescuer's assurance seemed to give her the courage to move forward. She'd learned to be self-reliant early in life, but the strength of this man seemed to flow into her body as he gave her his full attention. He walked slowly, and she struggled along beside him. When they came in sight of Biltmore, she was walking with only a slight limp in spite of the pain.

"If you need my support, I'll help you on to the house," Allen suggested. "But if you'd rather not have everyone know you had a fall, perhaps you'll want to go on by yourself."

"I am a little embarrassed to have been so careless," she answered, "so let me try to walk without your help. I know George Vanderbilt and my father well enough to realize that they'd make a big to-do over this and would probably call in a doctor to treat me. I don't need a doctor."

He removed his arm, and she took a few tentative steps alone. Although it was painful, Dora decided that she could manage. "I'll soak my foot in hot water and have my maid bandage it. Maude has been my maid since I was a child, and she shares most of my secrets."

"I'll watch until you reach the house. If you need help, motion to me and I'll come."

Allen watched Dora until she reached the mansion before he continued walking through the forest, marking trees he considered possibilities for harvesting. His mind, however, was wayward, and he kept thinking about Dora. Although their paths had never crossed, he'd heard of her beauty and charming ways, mostly in an article in the local newspaper announcing the visit of "Oliver Porter, New York billionaire, and his only daughter, Dora." If anyone had ever been born with "a silver spoon in her mouth," it would be Dora Porter.

Although he knew that Dora and her father were guests of George Vanderbilt and his mother, it hadn't entered his mind that he'd meet her. Besides having met her, he hadn't thought that a chance meeting with her would linger in his mind. He was disgusted with himself for succumbing to the charisma of Dora Porter.

Most of the local residents were overjoyed because the Vanderbilt family had changed Asheville from a sleepy mountain town to a mecca where rich

people would come to congregate year-round to escape the cold weather in winter or the sultry city
heat during the summer months. Allen, however,
was not pleased. When he'd bought property near the
small mill town of Fairfield, he hadn't dreamed that
the influence of the Vanderbilt family would draw
visitors from throughout the Northeast. Allen liked
solitude, which contributed to peace of mind. Having a tourist attraction like the Vanderbilt mansion
would bring too many visitors to the area. Already
the population of Asheville had increased percep-
tibly. He'd thought often of leaving the East and
traveling farther west, perhaps even to the Pacific
Coast, and he wondered if this was the time to leave
North Carolina.

As Allen headed northward in his buggy the next
day, considering the fact that he couldn't stop thinking about Dora, he wondered if he would ever have
peace of mind again. In his more than thirty years,
Allen hadn't been interested in women in general
and certainly none in particular. Why, of all people,
had he become infatuated with a woman as far out
of his reach as the North Pole?

The kind of life he envisioned for himself didn't
include a wife. He had left South Carolina when he
was a youth and cast his lot with the people who'd
established the mountainous community of Canaan,
North Carolina. After living in the area for several

years, he'd decided that Asheville would offer more advantages for him to prosper. He hadn't had a pleasant childhood, and considering the marital hardships of his parents, he didn't intend to establish a home and family of his own. He'd never met any woman who caused him to wonder if the single life wasn't all that he needed.

How could spending one evening in Dora's company make him realize how wrong he'd been?

When he had received the invitation from the Vanderbilts for the Biltmore dedication, he had tossed the invitation aside, having no intention of attending. He knew he'd be a fish out of water at the reception that would doubtless have several millionaires, as well as the elite of Asheville. He figured he would have nothing in common with the other guests, although he had heard that the Vanderbilts had extended a blanket invitation to anyone to come. However, when he'd met George Vanderbilt on the street shortly after and he had extended a verbal invitation, Allen knew he would have to attend. Mr. Vanderbilt had paid him handsomely for the work he had done at Biltmore during the mansion's construction, and it was obvious that the man wanted him at the party. And his Canaan cousin, Marie Bolden, had requested he escort her and a friend from Asheville. Marie's parents had been good to him when he was a youth. The least he could do was be her escort. So he wore the best suit he owned and went.

Now he wished he hadn't attended the Biltmore dedication at all. He didn't think it likely that in the large crowd he would even come face-to-face with Dora or that she would even recognize him. So he was surprised when she had made an effort to single him out at the party. With all the other men of her own class attending the big celebration, why had she chosen to spend most of the day with him? It had puzzled him throughout the night.

Allen looked with disfavor on his petite young cousin, Marie, who sat beside him. She kept talking about Biltmore and what a good time she'd had the day before. She must have become aware that he was displeased with her when she asked, "What's causing that scowl on your face?"

"I didn't realize my face was any different from usual."

Marie laughed. "Well, it looks like a thundercloud, and I can't figure out why. You monopolized the belle of the ball yesterday. You should be happy, happy, happy this morning."

He smiled slightly. "You always have been a nosy brat. I didn't sleep much last night, so don't pick at me this morning."

Marie was always a person who sensed when others were downhearted, but judging from the humor mirrored in her eyes, she didn't realize how the hours he'd spent in the presence of Dora, a New York socialite, had changed his life. Allen had always considered himself immune from attractive women, but he'd overestimated his willpower. After he'd helped Dora in the forest, he had supposed she'd returned to New York, and he doubted that he'd ever see her again. Then yesterday he'd gone to that dedication. His first glimpse of Dora had hit him like a bolt of lightning. During the time they'd spent together, she'd made it fairly evident that she intended to keep in touch with him.

"I'm sorry," Marie said. "I was pleased to see you enjoying yourself."

Allen doubted that she was sorry. Marie had pestered him since she was old enough to toddle around the house. Although he hadn't lived with her parents, they'd treated him like a son, and he'd been at their home quite often.

"Oh well, forget it."

"I figured you'd be in a good humor this morning. Dora Porter is one of New York City's most illustrious women, and you had the privilege of spending most of the day with her. I understand she's not easily attracted to men, but you seemed to be an exception." She smiled slyly. "In fact, I thought I heard you arrange to accompany her on a horseback ride into the mountains tomorrow."

He scowled at Marie, thankful that she hadn't heard about his rescue of Dora. Apparently Dora hadn't told anyone about their encounter, and he certainly had no intention of mentioning it. Actually, it was such a precious memory to him that he didn't want to share it with anyone.

"I might remind you that it isn't nice to eavesdrop, but it was a foolish thing for me to do. The way she was decked out in diamonds and other finery, it's obvious I can't afford her company. I'll have to send word that I can't keep the appointment."

Marie grinned widely. "Coward."

"And another thing—don't ask me to take you to Biltmore again," Allen said. "If they have another party, your brother can escort you."

"You know very well that Earl won't go. He's more interested living in that mountain cabin of his, pretending he's a frontiersman, than to associate with his family."

Allen didn't answer, and Marie sighed, wondering why she and her brother were so different. She'd always heard that most twins were inseparable, but that certainly wasn't true of Earl and herself.

They passed through Canaan, which had grown considerably from the small village that Vance Bolden had established twenty years ago. It was still a small town, where everyone knew everyone else, so they waved and called greetings to all visible residents. Canaan hadn't changed much since Allen had left it three years ago.

Leaving town, they turned south from Canaan

and followed a creek valley for about a mile when they rounded a curve in the road and Sunrise Manor came into view. A square two-story brick dwelling, the home of Vance and Evelyn Bolden, stood on a hill above the creek. Eight shuttered windows dominated the front of the house, and a small portico covered the massive front wooden door. Dry leaves from the two towering maple trees in front of the house littered the ground. A white picket fence surrounded a lawn, and a large barn and other outbuildings were located on a hill behind the house. Allen had come to this area as a boy, and here he'd grown to manhood. But he'd never seemed to fit into the society of Canaan, so he'd moved farther south.

As they approached the lawn, Jasper, a caretaker of the property, came out to take charge of their horses. A tall, well-built man stepped out of the front door and waved a hand in greeting. Vance Bolden's hair had turned gray, and he had put on some extra pounds, but he was still the same vibrant, authoritative man who'd led a wagon train of settlers from South Carolina to Canaan in 1875. Marie jumped from the buggy and rushed to her father. He picked her up and spun her around a couple of times.

"I've missed you, Daddy," she said.

"Same with your mother and me, but did you have a good time? That's all that matters."

"I did," Marie assured him. "It must be nice to have enough money to live in a house like Biltmore and to throw a party that hundreds of people attended." She looked around the yard, at the view of the mountains to the west, and when her mother stepped out of the house, she said, "But I wouldn't trade what we have for all the money in the world."

Evelyn Bolden hugged her daughter. "When I hear you make a remark like that, I know your father and I brought you up as you should be."

"By the way," Marie said, "all the Asheville cousins send their love. They were so nice to me."

Evelyn turned toward the front door. "Come in the house. Fannie just took a pan of gingerbread from the oven, so let's have a snack."

As he entered the home, Allen marveled at this woman who still treated him like family. In spite of a disastrous shipwreck that had almost taken her life, she had adjusted well to her new life in the United States. Her light hair had not turned gray, she was still slender, and the strength of her character had only grown stronger through the years. Although his biological parents still lived in South Carolina, Evelyn Bolden was the one who had "mothered" him.

Sometimes he wondered if he should return to his birthplace for a visit, but the longer he lived here, the farther away his old home seemed. He wasn't a rich man by any means, but he owned his own farm, free from debt, made an adequate living with his carpentry work, and belonged to a church where the pastor fed his soul each Sunday when he expounded on the Word of God. He hadn't possessed any of those things in his childhood home. No! He had all he needed.

Chapter 2

Dora's eyes widened at her father's words. Although she knew Oliver Porter wasn't given to levity, she did wonder if she'd heard him correctly.

"What did you say?"

They were sitting alone in a large room at Biltmore when Oliver handed her a brown envelope. "Happy birthday," he said.

Speechless, Dora stared at him.

"Your twenty-eighth birthday is next week, isn't it?" he prompted.

"Well, yes," she answered. "But you haven't remembered my birthday for a long time."

An expression, which was more like a smirk than

a smile, spread across his face. "I know I've been lax in my attentions, but I'm making up for it now. Here, take it!" he said, pushing the envelope into her hand.

Her father had hardly acknowledged her birthdays, so little wonder that his sudden change of heart surprised her.

"It isn't polite to refuse a gift. I'm your father; I want to give gifts to you."

"Thank you," she answered, wondering what his ulterior motive was.

"I'm making up for my neglect," he said. "I've bought complete ownership of a textile mill here in Asheville, and I had the deed made out to you. George Vanderbilt knew that I was interested in buying property in this state, and he notified me that the Fairfield Textile Mill was for sale. That's the reason I paid him a visit. I'm too busy with my New York and New England investments to manage this plant, but the price was reasonable and the mill is making quite a lot of money. It's a good investment. I expect you to live here and operate this business as if you were my son."

To a young woman who'd lived all of her life in New York City, such a statement seemed like being banished to a desert island. It had never been any secret that her father resented the fact that she was a female instead of the son who'd died in infancy. As if that was her fault! When he was so upset because she wasn't a boy, she'd often wondered why he hadn't married again after her mother had died giving birth to her. Still, he'd loved her mother devotedly and apparently not even for the possibility of a son would he have taken another wife. Instead, he'd tried to mold Dora into a boy. As she'd matured, Dora became known as one of the most attractive and eligible women in New York. But apparently her father still had hopes that she would take more interest in his wealth and business affairs. However, she'd never dreamed that he would carry his aspirations for her to this level.

"Father, you can't be serious! I don't know anything about operating a textile mill. I'd bankrupt the place before a year was out. If you want this mill, surely there are qualified local men who could be the manager."

"Yes, I'm searching for one. In the meantime, I've hired a local man to get the mill in the shape it needs to be. The mill has great possibilities, but the previous owner let the place run down. George Vanderbilt recommended Allen Bolden, a carpenter, who has done a lot of work at Biltmore. He's also worked at the textile mill. He's on good terms with the people who work in the plant. I went to his farm and talked with him today and asked him to become general manager. He absolutely refused, but he finally agreed to take care of the maintenance work on a six-month basis and that he would advise you if you had questions. I believe he has the know-how to get you started here. He's a smart man and can teach you the ins and outs of this business. I don't doubt that the two of you can work together and make this the best plant in the South."

Although Dora was irritated at her father for forcing her into a situation without even asking her consent, she could think of worse things than to be associated in a business venture with Allen Bolden. The man had made a favorable impression on her—a situation she hadn't experienced before. If she was forced into ownership of a textile mill, she couldn't think of anyone she'd rather have working with her, but it was by far the most ridiculous idea her father had sprung on her yet. Besides, she had a feeling that Allen wouldn't like having a woman for his boss. The possibility of seeing more of Allen intrigued her, but it still angered her that her father took her for granted.

"Father, do you think it's fair that you made all these plans without even consulting me? I've lived in New York all my life, and you're expecting me to pull up roots and spend the rest of my life here."

As usual he didn't try to justify his actions, but continued talking as if she hadn't spoken. "You don't get ahead in this world by always being fair. This is a big opportunity for us. It will be April before I get control of the plant. That will give you several months to get used to the idea."

Dora didn't answer him. If she had a few months,

she might convince her father that she wasn't suited for the work. Since her father was leaving for New York today, she was glad now that she'd let Mrs. Vanderbilt persuade her to spend a few more weeks with them. She didn't want her father to suspect her interest in Allen and that she was pleased to have more time with him.

Compared to men all over the world who'd tried to win her affection, she wondered why she favored Allen. She'd been pursued by some of the most eligible men without becoming interested in any of them. What was it about Allen that kept him constantly on her mind? Of medium height, he wasn't a particularly handsome man, but his wide shoulders and rugged appearance contributed to the strength and vitality that seemed to emanate from him like bolts of lightning. Perhaps it was the ready smile that caused his deep-set brown eyes to sparkle when he was amused. She had a feeling, however, that when he was crossed, those same eyes could blaze with anger and determination. Being honest with herself, she had a feeling that she was drawn to him in part because he seemed oblivious to her charm and beauty, which most men raved about.

In spite of being irritated because he'd fallen under the spell of Dora Porter, Allen couldn't stop thinking of her. His sleep had been troubled with dreams about her, and the morning passed slowly as he waited until he could see her again. Soon after noon, he chose two of his thoroughbred horses from the stable of the small farm he owned on the outskirts of Fairfield. Riding his favorite mare and leading Dora's mount, he rode through town.

Fairfield was much like a few other mill towns Allen had visited. Thomas McCallum, the first owner, had been concerned about the welfare of the mill people. He had provided attractive houses set off by lawns, hedges, and flowers. He maintained a community center and a farm that furnished villagers with fresh eggs, milk, chickens, and vegetables. However, the current owner of the textile mill had let working and housing conditions degrade. His ultimate concern for maximizing profits had led Fairfield from a clean, modest community to a run-down area in desperate need of improvement and repair.

A man with a deep Christian faith, Allen was pleased that a church had been established several years before the textile mill was built, when there were only a few residents in the area. Most of the newcomers were happy that the church provided a spiritual home for them and their families—it was one attribute that drew workers to the community.

The houses were mostly one-story cottages, although a few of the residents had two-story dwellings. He was somewhat surprised when he learned from George Vanderbilt that the new owner was intending to make many changes in the mill operation. He prayed that it would be a blessing to the employees rather than make their workload heavier.

The main road bypassed Fairfield and passed through the neighboring town of Asheville, which Allen followed and approached Biltmore from the south. A maid welcomed him to a porch on the rear of the mansion, where he waited until Dora joined him. He noticed a slight limp, but her face was animated, so he assumed that her injury wasn't causing much trouble. At least riding a horse wouldn't be difficult for her, and he wondered if she had looked forward to this afternoon as much as he had.

They headed northwest from the Biltmore Estate, riding single file until the trail widened. Surprised that he had become so quickly attuned to her moods, Allen sensed a difference in Dora. She wasn't the vivacious woman he'd met a few days ago. Was she sorry she'd agreed to go riding with him? Probably not, since she had greeted him warmly and smiled at him when he'd helped her into the saddle. Still, her expression seemed strained.

When the trail widened and they could ride side by side, he halted his horse until she caught up with him. Then he followed a trail that would take them closer to the mountains.

Dora rode in silence beside him for a few miles before she sighed. "I'm sorry I'm not very good company today."

Hesitantly, he asked, "Do you want to talk about

it? I'm a good listener, but I don't usually offer advice." He paused. "Unless I'm asked for it," he added with a slight smile.

Dora still seemed lost in her personal thoughts. "I should be used to it by now," she said bitterly, "but my father dominates my life. I'm almost twenty-eight years old, and at times he treats me like a child. Do you know that he's bought the Fairfield Textile Mill?"

"Yes, of course. I do their carpentry work, and I was there repairing some stair steps this morning. That's all anyone could talk about."

"Well, in a few months, they're going to have a new boss."

Surprised, he asked, "Who?"

"You're looking at her!"

Momentarily speechless, Allen couldn't imagine why Dora would be distressed by her father's gift. He couldn't think of any business he would rather own than the local textile mill. "And you don't want the mill?"

"Of course not! I've lived in New York all my life. And while I consider this a wonderful area for a vacation, I don't want to live here. If he'd just given me a choice in the matter, I might have agreed, but he makes decisions for me as if I'm a child. Right now I can't think of anything I'd like less than to own a textile mill."

They had reached an open place with a vivid view

of purple-hued mountains to the west, and he halted his horse. "Shall we stop for a while? We can talk some more."

"Yes, please," she said. "I'm too upset to be handling a horse anyway."

Allen helped her dismount and tied the horses in a small patch of vegetation where they could graze. She sat on a rock outcropping, and he reclined on the ground beside her.

Hesitantly, he said, "I think it's only fair to tell you that you won't be the only one upset."

"What do you mean?"

"I mean many people who work at the mill might be superstitious about having a woman as their boss."

"Including you?"

"I don't know," he admitted with a shrug of his shoulders. "If the boss is you, I probably wouldn't mind, but it would take some getting used to."

Even knowing how inferior his circumstances were to the way she'd lived all of her life, he was already attracted to her. It wouldn't be pleasant for him to have her as his employer. He'd thought that she would soon return to New York, and he wouldn't see her again—that he'd eventually forget her, which would be best for him. It would be disastrous for him to have her living in the area where he would see her often. Already he was attracted to her more than any woman he'd ever met. He didn't believe that he was in love with her—he hadn't known her long enough for that—but he didn't trust his emotions if he saw her often.

"You surely don't think I'd want to boss a bunch of men!"

She spat the words out as if it left a bitter taste in her mouth. Amused in spite of himself, and wondering why she disliked men, he said, "There are women as well as men who work in the mill, and I've known you long enough to believe that you can do anything you want to do. But you don't have to do what he says, do you?"

"No, but he hinted that he'd disinherit me if I refused his offer."

When they'd met at Biltmore, he had learned that she was an only child. "I doubt he'd treat you that way. With the money he apparently has, I wouldn't think you'd want his riches to go elsewhere."

Dora shrugged. "Oh, I don't know. He has a nephew, Blake Porter, who has tried for years to ingratiate himself into Father's business affairs. Father has always resented that I wasn't a boy. In a fit of anger, he might very well disinherit me and give his estate to Blake. That isn't as bad as it sounds because my maternal grandmother provided for me in her will, so I wouldn't be destitute. Being disinherited doesn't bother me that much—I've had proposals from some of the richest men in the country, so if all else failed, I could get married. I don't know what to do."

Allen couldn't understand why she hadn't married long ago. He considered the best way to advise her. "When I have a difficult decision to make, I turn to a higher power. Have you prayed about the situation?"

Dora stared at him. "Prayed!"

"Sure. I start every day asking God to guide my decisions and all else that I do. Isn't prayer a part of your life, too?"

She laughed. "Gracious, no! My father has endowed a church in New York City with money through the years, but that's the extent of our connection with religion. He contributes money to large churches with influential members because he thinks it will benefit him in the long run. But we never go to worship services." With a sinking heart, Allen said, "Then you don't believe in God?"

Dora gazed at the spectacular mountains in the distance. "Oh, I don't know. I can't believe that all of this beauty just happened, but I don't know which god was responsible for it."

Allen prayed that he would find the correct words. "There's only one God."

Dora shrugged. "I've traveled over a great part of the world, and I've seen altars and shrines to many gods."

At a loss to know how to respond, Allen didn't

comment. He would need to spend a lot of time in prayer to know how to point her in the right direction.

Immediately Dora sensed that Allen was distressed about her comments, which distressed *her*. Indeed, it was beyond her wildest imagination to comprehend why she felt so drawn to Allen Bolden. As far as she could determine, they had nothing in common. She had lived all her life in a metropolitan area. He was "country" through and through. Now it seemed that he was a spiritual man, and her father was an atheist. What kind of religion did she have? Very little, if any. She admitted that when she'd traveled to the scenic areas of Europe or had looked upon the grandeur of the mountains in the northeast United States, she'd wondered somewhat about creation. Her maid, Maude, was a Christian, and she'd tried to influence Dora's beliefs, but her words had fallen on deaf ears when she'd witnessed about her faith to Dora.

She'd often heard that opposites attracted one another. Was that true?

Suddenly aware that she'd been so busy with her thoughts that she'd forgotten her companion, Dora felt her face flushing.

"But back to my current decision," she said quickly. "I told Father I don't want the responsibility of the mill, but as usual, he won't listen to me, so I haven't heard the last of the subject. It doesn't seem to occur to him that I would be completely out of place in a rural setting like this. It's been interesting to come to Asheville for a short time, but I can't imagine spending the rest of my life in North Carolina."

Allen sensed that she was more or less talking to herself, that she didn't want an answer, so he remained silent.

"You're the only friend I've made here. If I'm forced to do what Father says, will you work for me—be the general manager of the mill? I won't interfere with your decisions."

Allen doubted that statement, but he didn't comment on it. At this point, he wasn't the least bit interested in her offer. He didn't know what he might do in the future, but that would be soon enough to set up some rules if he agreed to work for her. "Would you stay in Asheville or would you return to New York?"

"Oh, I'd have a residence here to satisfy Father's demands, but I'd probably spend most of my time in New York."

"That's just what I suspected." Without hesitation, Allen said dogmatically, "I'm a carpenter, not a textile mill worker. I haven't had any experience managing anything except my own personal affairs. I wouldn't take responsibility of running the mill unless the owner is on hand to oversee the work. Living conditions are not as bad as the few mills I've visited, but if I were the manager, I'd probably want to improve on their lifestyle—give them more time off, bonuses for good work, and make their lives as happy as possible. You've never supervised a group of workers, so the workers might take advantage of your lack of experience. I'd be honest with you, but some men wouldn't. It's unreasonable for your father to force you into this position, but it seems you don't have much choice. Accept the mill or lose your inheritance?"

She shrugged. "That's what he threatened."

"If he's that kind of scoundrel," Allen continued, "then you'd be better off to let him cut you off without a penny now and stop depending on him. However, I figure he's bluffing. You've indicated that he's always tried to dominate you, so he won't give up easily. Frankly, I think it would be good for you to stay in North Carolina for a few months and see how the rest of the world lives."

"I don't have to make a decision now. As I understand, the present manager is retiring due to ill health, but we won't gain possession of the mill until April. I'm returning to New York soon. It's a big decision to make."

"In the meantime, I'd suggest that you take a tour of the mill and the towns of Asheville and Fairfield before you decide on anything."

"I'm sorry to impose on you, but will you go with

me through the mill? I feel as if I've known you a long time, and I trust you."

Her comment surprised as well as pleased Allen. He wondered how she could have formed a favorable opinion of him in such a short time. "When are you leaving for New York?"

"I was to leave with Father yesterday, but the Vanderbilts have insisted that I should remain another week or so, and I've decided to stay."

"I'm doing some carpentry work at the mill. I go in after the plant closes for the night. I could come to Biltmore to get you Monday afternoon around five o'clock. The manager takes himself seriously, so he may not want you on the premises during work hours. But as the new owner of the mill, you certainly have the right to look over your property. You're sure the transaction has already taken place?"

"Father said the papers have been signed and a down payment made. The ownership passes to me in two months. Father has his faults, but he never lies, so I know that's the way it's going to be."

"I wouldn't mention to anyone around here that you're going to own the plant. I figure some of the workers would be superstitious about a woman boss, so it will be good for them to see you *before* they know you're the new owner. Any change in ownership of a business scares the employees. Wages are low and most of them live from hand-to-mouth, and they face starvation if a business closes. If you'll take my advice, I think you should see the mill before you go. Tomorrow is Sunday, and there won't be many people at the plant. It might be better to go then. I'll be glad to be your guide."

Hesitantly, she agreed to his plan. "What time should I be ready?"

"I attend worship services at Bethel Community Church in Fairfield on Sunday morning. If you'd like to go with me, I'll come by for you at nine o'clock. We can tour the mill after that and eat our dinner at Aunt Sallie's Boardinghouse."

She shook her head, and a determined expression crossed her face. "I won't go to church, but I'd like to tour the mill and eat at Aunt Sallie's. I've noticed her quaint little cottage, and I've thought it would be interesting."

Although Allen was disappointed at her response, he wasn't surprised. He'd been in her presence enough to know that she was strong-willed, obviously a trait she'd inherited from her father. That was all right. He also had a stubborn streak, and he vowed silently that if Dora stayed in North Carolina, he would eventually see her converted to the same faith he followed. Stubborn streak or not, he was in the winner's seat because he had God on his side. One of the Bible references he quoted often was from the book of Romans, "If God be for us, who can be against us?"

Allen was distressed about his interest in Dora,

and he knew that if he didn't depend on God for direction, he'd say or do something that would betray that interest to her. In spite of all her wealth and prestige, he sensed that inwardly Dora wasn't happy. He would like to help her, but could he do that without endangering his own heart?

Although he knew there were too many barriers between Dora and himself for them to be anything more than friends, Allen wanted very much for her to share his Christian faith. At least their lives could be joined together in a spiritual sense. He would never be satisfied until he knew that Dora believed in and worshipped the same God he did. Although he'd felt this way about the eternal destiny of many people, for some reason Dora's salvation seemed more important than any other's right now.

Mentally, he placed his concern before God, and reminded himself that with God all things were possible. *"If ye have faith as a grain of mustard seed, ye shall say unto this mountain, Remove hence to yonder place; and it shall remove."*

Chapter 3

Bethel Community Church had at one time been a country church, established by an itinerant preacher, Jeremiah Spencer, whose Christian calling had been to gather a congregation in an area that didn't have a house of worship. Although Asheville had several churches, none had been built in the town of Fairfield until Reverend Spencer arrived. The church had originally been a log structure, but it had been covered with weather boarding two years ago. The organist was playing the introductory music to "Rock of Ages" when Allen entered the building. He moved into the left rear seat, took a hymnal from the rack, and joined the singing.

"Rock of Ages, cleft for me,
let me hide myself in Thee;
let the water and the blood,
from Thy wounded side which flowed,
be of sin the double cure;
save from wrath and make me pure."

The preacher's text for his sermon was taken from
the fourth Psalm, when David had said, "I will both
lay me down in peace, and sleep: for thou, Lord, only
makest me dwell in safety."

As Reverend Spencer presented his carefully prepared message emphasizing the watchful care of
the heavenly Father, Allen recalled one of the most
frightening experiences of his youth. He and one of
his younger brothers had been fishing from a boat in
a creek that flowed into the Atlantic Ocean not far
from the city of Charleston. The water was smooth,
and the weather was peaceful. Suddenly the water
roiled around the inlet, and an offshore tidal wave
forced itself over the peaceful waters of the creek.
The canoe capsized, and his brother sank out of
sight. Knowing that the child couldn't swim, Allen,
praying continually, kept diving until he found his
brother and hauled him to safety.

It was one of Allen's most poignant memories. In
spite of the fact that he'd saved the boy's life, when
they returned to their home, his parents had heaped
recriminations on Allen because he'd put the boy

in such a dangerous situation. That was the time Allen had made up his mind to leave South Carolina and, at the age of fifteen, he joined his cousin Vance Bolden's caravan and moved to North Carolina. That had been years ago, and he hadn't seen any of his family since. Timothy would be a young man by now, and he wondered what had happened to the boy.

As he listened to the pastor's message, and thinking of Dora's situation, he wondered if his reaction to his parents' rejection was any worse than what she was facing just now. Perhaps if he could direct her to a better relationship between herself and her father, he might learn how to deal with memories of his family and the past.

When he reached Biltmore, Dora and George Vanderbilt were seated on one of the enclosed porches, and George walked to the buggy with Dora. Although Mr. Vanderbilt had never appeared condescending to Allen, he still felt inferior to the man. And why wouldn't he? The Vanderbilt family was one of the most prosperous and prestigious families in the world. Allen had neither wealth nor prestige. His personal assets amounted to a few thousand dollars, and it had taken a lifetime to accumulate that. Furthermore, his parents had been sharecroppers on a farm near Charleston, and there wasn't any prestige in that occupation.

And you're foolish enough to keep company with

a woman whose father is probably as rich as George Vanderbilt, he castigated himself. Although Dora didn't seem condescending to him, what could she see in him? Just somebody to break the monotony of a trip to the mountains?

"How do you like the news that Dora is soon to be owner of the local textile mill?" George asked when he reached the buggy. That comment didn't do anything to make Allen not consider his inferior standing compared to the Porters and Vanderbilts!

Allen secured the reins of the horses and stepped out of the buggy to shake hands with Vanderbilt. He forced a smile. "I have a feeling it will take a while for the workers to grow accustomed to the change, but I'm sure Miss Porter is capable of handling the business."

"With your help, my good man. With your help! She's counting on you."

Allen considered Vanderbilt a pompous man, and he was uneasy in his presence, so he turned his attention to Dora. Without commenting on Vanderbilt's suggestions, Allen took her arm and helped Dora to settle on the buggy's seat. He joined her, untied the reins, and lifted his left hand in a farewell gesture to Vanderbilt.

"I don't know how long it will take us to tour the mill," Dora said to George, "but I'm sure I'll be in good hands."

"We'll be back before nighttime," Allen called as

he guided the horses around the circular drive and headed toward Asheville.

"You probably sensed that George isn't favorable to the idea that I'll own the mill, and he likes to joke about it," Dora said. "I had supposed Father would have asked his advice about the purchase and his subsequent plans to give the mill to me." She frowned. "Apparently that wasn't the case, and Father went his own way as usual."

"So you've decided to take over management of the mill?"

"I've lost a lot of sleep worrying about it, and I've concluded that I don't have much choice. To be honest, all my life I've had almost anything I wanted handed to me on a silver platter. I've never worked for anything. I've 'played' most of my life. I actually think that Father doesn't expect me to be able to operate the mill, so I have an ulterior motive. I'm going to accept ownership of the mill just to show Father that I can do it. I suppose it boils down to the fact that I want to prove to myself as well as to him that I'm capable of operating a business."

As she talked, Allen's heart warmed and he said encouragingly, "There isn't a doubt in my mind that you can manage the mill."

She touched his right hand where he held the reins. "But only if you'll help me."

"I'll help you," Allen agreed. It wasn't something he was deciding on the spur of the moment. In their short acquaintance, he'd decided that Dora had the temperament to accomplish anything she wanted to do. He'd already decided that if Dora asked for his help again, she'd get it so he didn't hesitate in promising to advise her.

"I'll want you to tell me when I'm wrong and give me advice. I may not like it, but I know I can't do it without you."

"I'll do anything I can, but I'm not a businessman or a miracle worker. However, now that you want my advice, I'm telling you that unless you're ready to devote one hundred percent of your time to the mill, you should tell your father to forget it. I suggest that you wait until you have a tour of the mill and see what you're up against before you make your final decision. You're going to witness 'life's other side' this afternoon."

Dora looked at him with an incredulous expression on her face, but she didn't comment as they headed toward the small village. When they reached the outskirts of Fairfield, Allen slowed the horses. Smiling, he said, "I know this town can't compare with the cities you've seen, but I'll take you on a tour of Fairfield. On the left is the textile mill you will soon own."

"Gracious! It's a rather shabby building, and a big one."

Allen shrugged his shoulders. "All textile mills look like that. There are large fans in the ceilings to blow the lint and other elements that gathered in the air through high windows in the structure." Driving slowly, he pointed out a few of the other landmarks, including a brick church with a tower.

"That's Bethel Community Church, which I attended this morning. It's been here longer than the town itself. The church was established about fifty years ago, and this was all country then. The textile mill was built ten years later, and the town grew up around it."

Many people were strolling along the tree-shaded streets, evidently enjoying the sun and the invigorating breeze wafting down from the mountains. Most of them waved, and Allen returned the salute.

"Twenty acres of forest were cleared for the construction of the mill," Allen explained as he tightened the reins and brought the team of Morgan horses to a slow walk. "The lumber was used to build the town itself. I lived in the town of Canaan, several miles north of here, but I'm a carpenter, and I came here to help build the houses and mill. I didn't necessarily intend to stay after the mill was in operation, but I like it here, so I've stayed on." When they passed Aunt Sallie's Boardinghouse, Allen said, "That's where I lived until I saved enough money to buy a small farm outside of town. I have a small cabin on the land now."

From the puzzled expression on Dora's face, Allen suspected that he might as well be talking a foreign language, so he added, "When I came to North Carolina, where my cousin established the village of Canaan, he distributed land to his friends and neighbors who had traveled with him. I could have had a parcel of land in that settlement, but I didn't want to be a farmer. So I became a self-taught carpenter and helped build the little town."

"But you're a farmer now."

"I own a small farm, but I prefer building things with my hands rather than tilling the soil. That's one reason I didn't get along with my father. He wanted me to work for him on the plantation near Charleston. I couldn't see any future there because many residents were still living in the past—thinking that the old carefree days prior to the War Between the States would return. I didn't think that was going to happen; besides I prefer to look toward the future instead of dwelling on the past."

"But you like it here and intend to stay?"

"So far. I've never put down roots anywhere, so I don't know. Farming is sort of a hobby for me. As far as I'm concerned, it's a poor way to make a living, but combining that with carpentry, I'm doing all right."

When they reached the mill, Allen secured the buggy and horses then helped Dora to the ground. He opened the huge metal doors and motioned for her to precede him into the mill.

* * *

Dora's first impression of the textile mill was that the huge room was dark and dirty. She sneezed as Allen opened two other doors in addition to the one they'd entered.

"There's usually lint from the fabrics floating around this building. That's what caused the sneeze."

Inside, the building seemed even larger than it did from the outside, and numerous machines were situated around the room. Most of them had fabric of different kinds in the process of being woven. Large bolts of cotton were stored on shelves.

What a terrible place to work, she thought and wondered why her father had invested in the place. No doubt he'd been able to buy the mill at a low price and was convinced he could double his money in a short time. If she accepted this gift from him, she vowed to herself that she'd improve working conditions for her employees. She couldn't imagine what it would be like to work day after day in such a place.

Dora saw a figure coming toward them, and supposing it was a workman, she was surprised to see a young woman sweeping the floor.

"Kitty," Allen called. "We have company. Miss Porter is visiting in the area, and I brought her to see the mill. We can wait outside until you're finished."

"Ain't no need of that, Mister Allen. I'm almost through. Come on in."

The girl was of slight build, and Dora noticed

that she walked with a limp as she approached them. "Miss Porter, this is Kitty Franklin. Her mother is one of the mill employees. Her father died last year, and Kitty does odd jobs around the plant to help support the family."

A sense of frustration mixed with compassion swept through Dora's heart. Most of her life she'd heard the statement "life's other side." Allen had used it that very day. She believed she had seen the depth of that "other side" in the past few days, but this child's injury, her poor grammar, and her ragged garments reached a portion of Dora's heart that had never been stirred. Looking beyond the girl's disability, she realized that Kitty was really a beautiful girl. Was it conceivable that if she managed the mill she could make this girl's life happier? No doubt there were many such cases in these mountains where she could make a difference in the lives of those who weren't as fortunate as she'd been all of her life.

Unaccustomed to such feelings of frustration, she wished momentarily that she'd never met Allen Bolden or had ever come to North Carolina. As long as she had stayed at Biltmore, her lifestyle didn't differ from what she'd always known. Her association with Allen, however, had introduced her to a segment of society that she didn't even know existed. Why had she ever made this trip to North Carolina? Her peace of mind had been disrupted, and for the first time she was dissatisfied with her own way of living.

"What's wrong with her leg?" she asked Allen after the girl left the building.

"As I understand, she broke her leg when she was three or four years old, and there wasn't any doctor available to take care of it."

"You mean there isn't a company doctor to minister to the workers in this mill or to their families?"

He shook his head. "There are doctors in Asheville, but most of our local residents doctor themselves. They can't afford to pay for health care. As for Kitty, it's not as bad as it sounds. For one thing, they didn't live here when the accident happened. Her parents moved from another village southeast of here. There's a doctor in Fairfield, as well as doctors in Asheville, who take care of the accidents that happen in the mill itself."

"Still, it seems harsh for the child to live like that."

"I agree. But some of these people have Calvinistic views—meaning that they believe whatever will be, will be, and they accept life as it is. They don't believe in doctoring."

As they walked around the large building, Allen explained the purpose of each machine to Dora, which gave her an idea of the output of the workers. She asked a few questions, but what impressed her most was not the mill products as much as the poor lighting and the dirt and dust on the machinery as well as the floor. How miserable it would be to spend six days working in such squalor!

They said good-bye to Kitty and left the building. "Any questions?" Allen asked as he took her arm and assisted her into the buggy.

"Yes, but one you probably can't answer. Why would my father be interested in buying a textile mill in North Carolina?"

"To make money," Allen said without hesitation. "The textile industry is one of the most lucrative businesses in the South now. The climate is perfect for growing cotton. There are hundreds of people, both men and women, who need employment and who will work long hours for low wages. It's a potential gold mine for someone who has plenty of money to invest. At Vanderbilt's request, I took your father on a tour of the village as well as the mill. He obviously knows a good deal when he sees it. There's money to be made here, and he wants the Porters to make that money. I observed him at Biltmore and when he toured this plant. He knows a good thing when he sees it."

"I still don't understand why he wants to give the mill to me. He's not an old man—he manages his other business investments."

Allen unhitched the horses and climbed into the buggy beside her. "Are you his only child?"

"Yes. My mother died giving birth to me. He's

lamented more than once that he wished I'd been a boy. I don't know why he didn't marry again and perhaps have a son." She shrugged and continued. "But it's a legend in our family that Porters only marry once. They marry for love, and it's a lifetime commitment."

Smiling at her, Allen said, "Does that apply to women as well as men?"

She favored him with an oblique glance. "I don't know from personal experience. I've never been in love."

As they left the mill behind, Allen sensed a lift of his spirits as he recalled her words. "If you aren't in any particular hurry, I'll take the long drive back to Biltmore after we eat at Aunt Sallie's."

"I'd like that! Since I'll be leaving for New York soon…"

He glanced quickly toward her. "Not to stay."

"If father carries through with his plans of giving the textile mill to me, I suppose I'll have to come here occasionally. However, I think you've been hinting that being an absentee landlord isn't a good thing."

"Now just a minute—don't blame me for the decisions you have to make. I've just answered your questions, but you've admitted that you wouldn't want to live here."

"That's true, but I've got a stubborn streak—apparently inherited directly from Father because my

mother's relatives aren't like that. I'd be willing to
bet the reason he bought the mill in the first place
was that he looked the situation over and decided a
lot of money could be made. He's determined that
I must earn any inheritance I get from him, and if
he makes me take this mill, I'm going to turn it into
the most successful textile mill in the state of North
Carolina without any help from him. The first thing
I'd do is improve the working conditions. Father
won't like that, though, because that would eat up
most of the profits."

"You can't do that by living in New York."

"Can you actually envision me living in Fairfield?"

Laughing, Allen said, "No, but I can't envision
you living in New York for that matter. An absentee
landlord can't give one hundred percent to his—or
her, in your situation—work. In my opinion, that's
necessary for success in the few businesses I've seen
operate. That's the reason the former owner didn't
make a profit. He lived in South Carolina and only
came here occasionally."

"I've never had any experience operating a business of any kind, so I'll probably spend as much
time here as I do in New York, at least until I learn
what it requires to own and operate a textile mill.
I've been discontented the last year or two, feeling
that I wasn't accomplishing anything, so perhaps
a new challenge is what I need. I'm determined to

make a success of this, if for no other reason than to prove my worth to Father. I can't do it alone, but I believe the two of us working as a team can make this a good investment. I may even take you in as a partner. Are you interested in managing the mill?"

He shook his head. "No, I wouldn't unless I had absolute control, and I know you well enough already to realize that you'll be determined to operate the business your own way. I don't blame you for that—that would be my attitude. I've got a stubborn streak, too," he said, and a determined expression spread across his face. "I'm not going to tie myself to any promises I don't want to keep."

"Well, we've laid the cards on the table, so to speak. I know what to expect from you—you know what to expect from me."

He lifted the reins, and the eager horses took off at a trot as soon as they reached the narrow road heading north. Neat farmsteads lined the road, but the owners and their farmhands alike were loafing as they took advantage of their one day of rest. In a small community like this, no one was a stranger, so Allen waved to everyone.

They rode for several miles without talking. Dora seemed satisfied to just look at the scenery, and he was pleased that she didn't find it necessary to carry on a conversation all the time. Another reason he admired Dora. Being a quiet person himself, he was often frustrated when he was in the company of someone who talked constantly. He was thankful for the opportunity to spend as much time with her as he could. The fact that she was returning to New York in a little while distressed him. When she reached New York and resumed the company of her former friends, mill or no mill, would she ever return to North Carolina? Although Dora seemed convinced that her father would disinherit her if she refused to accept ownership of the mill or couldn't operate it with a profit, Allen didn't think that would happen. Mr. Porter was a shrewd man, and he would prod her to be successful.

A sobering thought entered Allen's mind. What if Mr. Porter's next move was to coerce Dora into getting married to someone who was an expert in business management? As far as that was concerned, he couldn't understand why Dora wasn't already married, or at least engaged. He couldn't believe the men in New York wouldn't see what a wonderful woman she was. However, he was sure that Oliver Porter would be very selective in any man he would accept as a son-in-law.

Allen wouldn't ask her about any love affairs, of course, but it was difficult to believe that a woman as beautiful and personable as she was had not been married long before this. He realized that the best thing for him was to dismiss Dora and her problems from his mind, but that was easier said than done. Once she returned to New York, she would go out of his life, but that didn't make it any easier. It didn't take a fortune-teller for him to realize that he was getting too interested in a woman who was as far out of his reach as the moon and stars.

Chapter 4

The horses needed very little guidance, so Allen relaxed and enjoyed the ride. They had the countryside to themselves until they met a boy plodding along the side of the road, carrying a sack over his shoulder. Allen lifted his hand in greeting as he always did. The lad looked up briefly, but didn't return the greeting. Tightening the reins to slow the horses, Allen drove on a short distance before he halted the team.

"Something wrong?" Dora inquired.

"I don't know," Allen said slowly. He turned and looked at the young man they'd just met. "That boy reminded me of my father. In fact, from this angle, he still looks like my father. I remember that Pa often seemed that weary when he'd come home from work every day."

"I don't know your father, of course, but the boy does seem to have a deliberate way of walking just as you do."

Allen glanced her way in surprise. She would have had to study him intently to know that! Was it possible that a woman like Dora Porter could actually be interested in *him*? That the attraction he held for her wasn't just one-sided? *Nah!* he thought. *Don't flatter yourself!* Determined to convince himself that her attitude toward him was the friendliness she showed everyone, he considered again why she would have any interest in him except a pleasant interlude in the country.

Lifting the reins, Allen turned the team and headed back the way they'd come without commenting on her statement. When he drew up beside the walker, he stopped. The boy looked up, and Allen felt as if someone had sucker punched him. The boy resembled himself at that age.

Quietly, Dora said, "He looks like you, Allen. Is he a relative?"

He shrugged. "I don't know." Directing his attention to the boy, Allen asked, "Would you like a ride?"

"Maybe," the boy said, his dark brown eyes boring into Allen's. "Where you goin'?"

"Asheville. What's your name?"

The boy grinned slightly. "Timothy Bolden. What's yours?"

"Allen Bolden."

"Then you're my brother. I've been lookin' for you for months. I'd about given up."

Although it had been twenty years since Allen had left South Carolina, he didn't doubt that the boy was his brother. He had several Bolden traits that Allen had also inherited—wide shoulders, a legacy from their maternal grandfather—as well as the thick dark hair and piercing brown eyes of their mother's family.

"I set out about six months ago to see if I could find you. I'm actually on my way to California, but I wanted to see you once more. I figure if I go as far as the Pacific, I'll never come back this way again."

Allen handed the reins to Dora, vaulted out of the buggy, and grabbed his brother in a bear hug. A lump formed in his throat, and his eyes were misty. Although he had willingly severed ties with his family, at times he'd wondered about them, but not to the extent that he considered returning to South Carolina. He hadn't seen a close relative since the day he left home, but now he realized that some corner of his heart had cherished memories of his childhood.

"What about the family?"

"Ma died and Pa married again, a widow with five younguns. Our other brothers and sisters are married. I'm the youngest, and I didn't seem to fit in anywhere. I'd thought a lot about goin' west, maybe as far as California, so when I turned eighteen, I started out. As I moved westward, I took a job here and there till I had a little money to move on. I worked in Canaan for a few weeks and somebody told me where you were livin'. I decided to find you if I could before I left this part of the country." He glanced at Dora. "Is this your woman?"

Allen shook his head and smiled in Dora's direction. "She isn't anybody's 'woman.' She's a very nice lady, though. Timothy, meet Miss Dora Porter."

Dora smiled, but she didn't speak. Allen knew from the soft glow in her eyes that she'd been touched to see the reunion of the two brothers who'd been separated for years. No doubt she had often wished for siblings.

"Pleased to meet you, ma'am," Timothy said as he took off his cap.

Allen noticed that although Timothy's clothes were well-worn, he was clean and smoothly shaved, so he didn't think Dora would mind if he offered the boy a ride.

"I live near the town of Fairfield, where Miss Porter is visiting from New York. We're just out for a ride, so why don't you go into town with us and maybe stay a few days. I live on a small farm, and I've got an extra bed."

"Sounds good to me," Timothy said. "Now, mind, I'm not spongin' off you. I've got some money."

He hoisted himself to the back of the buggy. Allen resumed his seat and took the reins from Dora.

Allen had never missed the separation from his close relatives because Evelyn and Vance Bolden had treated him like family, always inviting him to holiday festivities at their home in Canaan. Furthermore, he had an open invitation to visit their home at anytime. After he'd moved to the Asheville area, though, he'd been a loner. He had a host of acquaintances, but not many close friends. It pleased him to meet this lad.

Perhaps sensing his churning emotions, Dora put her hand on his shoulder and left it there for several miles, but she didn't comment on the reunion. Contemplating the past he'd left behind, Allen didn't want to talk either.

They were almost to Biltmore when Dora broke the silence. "Since, like it or lump it, I've fallen heir to the textile mill, I should find a place of my own to live when I'm in North Carolina. George and his mother will probably insist that I stay at Biltmore, but I won't do that. I'd prefer to have a place of my own. Do you know of a small house I can rent?" Smiling, she added, "One that comes with a housekeeper? Maude will expect to take care of the house, but she'll have enough to do without that."

"I know of only one vacant house in Fairfield

that you'd even consider renting. Most of the other dwellings are small—probably about the size of a bedroom in your Long Island residence."

She poked him in the side with her elbow. "You're being sarcastic, aren't you?"

"Nope! Just speaking the truth. The house belongs to an elderly woman who's living with her daughter in Asheville now. She's an invalid, and it isn't likely she'll ever live in the house again. I doubt that she'd consider renting, but she might be willing to sell it. There isn't much rental property in Fairfield."

"I know you think I'm a spoiled brat, but I can't help my background any more than you had anything to do with where you were born and into what family. If I'd give all my money away, would you have more respect for me than you do now?"

Allen was struck speechless for a few moments, and he slowed the horses' gait by pulling the reins. "Now just a minute! What gave you the idea that I don't respect you?"

"You're critical of everything I say or do, and you act like it's a crime to live in New York." Her dark eyes flashed with anger, and long, mysterious, soaring eye-brows enhanced her curving eyelashes. He'd never seen a more beautiful woman. She was pretty enough when she was smiling, but now anger had unleashed a bewitching feminine charm he hadn't noticed before.

He cleared his throat and answered calmly, "I don't remember that I've ever criticized you unless you asked for my opinion. If you don't want the truth from me, don't ask me any questions."

"For your information, life here is as far removed from my lifestyle in New York as if I lived on an island in the Pacific." When he would have protested, she continued, "I live in an apartment. Our ancestral home along the Hudson River is huge, but I don't like to live there alone. Father is gone quite a lot, so I have an apartment in New York City, where I live most of the time. But I doubt there are any apartments to be had in Fairfield, so I thought I'd need a house. I'd prefer to buy one if I can't persuade Father to change his mind about giving the mill to me. Of course there's always the chance that I might make such a disaster of managing the business that he'll change his mind about having me as the resident proprietor."

Her great eyes glistened with unshed tears, and Allen was tempted to stop the buggy, take her in his arms, and comfort her. Then he remembered his brother. Instead he laughed. "I doubt that. From what I've observed in the few days I've known you, I believe you'll do everything in your power to make the business successful—just to prove to your father that you can. I don't doubt that you'll succeed, and although I usually tend to my own business, I am going to warn you that you shouldn't trust the present manager, Ted Morgan, too far."

Surprise was evident in her voice when she said, "I don't understand. Father said he was recommended by a business associate. He's been here a few months, I believe."

Allen shrugged. "It's just a hunch I have that he might not be too trustworthy. Also, being from New York, he doesn't understand the culture of the people here in the mountains. He's making them change their ways and habits. They don't like it. For instance, they're accustomed to a half-hour break in the morning and afternoon and an hour off for lunch. He's changed the schedule to two fifteen-minute breaks and forty-five minutes for lunch."

"I appreciate having you tell me that, and I'll watch him carefully."

"You can't do that from New York."

Dora appraised him with frank, speculative, dark eyes, but she didn't comment.

Chapter 5

Disgusted with himself because he kept coming up with ideas to keep Dora in North Carolina, Allen didn't say anything else. Instead, he wondered about Timothy. Although he was pleased to see the boy, he hardly knew what to do with him. Should he try to convince his brother to stay in North Carolina? He thought the boy was just asking for trouble to be wandering around the country alone. Since he was sixteen, Allen had been on his own, and from experience he'd learned that it wasn't an easy life.

Because Dora had mentioned buying a local home, he drove to a row of houses a mile or more from the mill and pointed out a house he thought

Dora could rent—a story-and-a-half frame dwelling in excellent condition with an inviting front porch. Flower beds in the front yard enhanced the beauty of the site. Since it was located several blocks from the textile mill, the noise wouldn't be too bothersome. Dora seemed pleased with the house and asked him to make arrangements for her to see the interior.

Allen agreed to do so, but he refused to accompany Dora when she asked him to go with her when she went to view the house.

"I'll get in touch with the owner and make an appointment for you to check out the property, but I won't go with you to look over the place. I don't want to influence your decision. What you like, I might not, and since you're the one who will be living there, you shouldn't be influenced by my opinion. I'm sure George Vanderbilt will be happy to go with you."

A half smile hovered on Dora's lips, and he wondered if she thought he was jealous of George. To his knowledge, George wasn't married, and since she was visiting there, no doubt the man would be romantically interested in Dora. He had a sinking feeling, knowing that a match between them was certainly possible. Both families had money and similar family backgrounds, so it wasn't unlikely.

Well, if that ever happened, he'd pull up stakes and head westward. Since he relied on God to direct his life, he couldn't help wondering why God had brought him into close contact with a woman like Dora. Ironically, he put a new twist on an old proverb. Instead of "East is east and west is west and never the twain shall meet," the proverb that described his relationship with Dora should be: "Rich is rich and poor is poor and never the twain shall meet."

After he had taken Dora through the small residential district of Fairfield, he said, "I'll drive you to Biltmore before I take Timothy out to the farm."

"How do you manage a farm and do carpentry work, too?" Dora asked.

"I'm not a farmer and never intend to be, but I needed a home, and I had an opportunity to buy this farm two years ago. It's only forty acres and mostly in pastureland. I have a small herd of cattle. The house is small, but it does have two bedrooms, so I have room for Timothy."

"You're happy about Timothy being here, aren't you?"

Quietly, he answered, "Yes, I didn't know how much I'd missed not having any family until I saw him. I'll not get too attached to him, though. If he's affected with wanderlust, he may soon get tired of Fairfield and start traveling again."

"If we give him a job at the cotton mill, he may decide to stay."

"That's possible. I'll mention it to him. When are you returning to New York?"

"Father has written that he wants me to come home next week. I must meet with his lawyer about transferring all his North Carolina assets to me." She paused and said with a sigh, "What would you do if you were given something you didn't want?"

"I can't tell you. Unless I've walked in your shoes, so to speak, I wouldn't know."

"You aren't much help," Dora said with a frown. "Just pretend that someone wanted to give you this mill. What would you do?"

Shrugging his shoulders, Allen said, "I wouldn't want to own a textile mill, so if it was mine, I'd sell it. However, your father hasn't given you that option. But if I were the owner, I'd turn it into the best textile mill in the country, and my first concern wouldn't be making money. I'd want good working conditions for the employees. I'd improve the company houses where most of the employees live. Because the houses aren't much good, the inhabitants don't make a lot of effort to keep them clean. It's my thought that if you put the employees' welfare first, they'll give you the best labor they can, and you'll make more money than if you tried to keep everything for yourself."

Dora looked at him, and Allen couldn't interpret the softening expression in her clear, steadfast eyes. Her eyes were luminous, and a slight flush spread across her face. She took a quick breath and looked away. "It's obvious you're a philanthropist."

"Well, I don't know what that big word means, but what did I say wrong?" Allen asked, puzzled by the change in her.

"Nothing's wrong," she said. "You're a good, amazing man, Allen Bolden. You'd inspire a mummy to become a better person."

Embarrassed by the change in Dora, Allen said, "The Bible says that we shouldn't call any person good. 'He hath shewed thee, O man, what is good; and what doth the Lord require of thee, but to do justly, and to love mercy, and to walk humbly with thy God?' That's what determines if we're a good person."

Dora frowned. "Gracious! I pay you a compliment, and you preach a sermon. You're a difficult man to understand."

While Allen refused to accompany Dora when she went to view the brick house she considered buying, George Vanderbilt was glad to go with her. Indeed, he volunteered to go. Maude also went with them. The house was small, but it reminded Dora of the home her family had owned along the Atlantic Coast when she was a child. In addition to the master bedroom with an adjacent bathroom, two smaller bedrooms and a bathroom had been built on the opposite side of the house. Maude was more aware of what they needed in a home than Dora was, so she relied on her companion's comments in deciding to buy or rent it.

Separating the bedroom wings was a great room and a kitchen with a small dining nook. Compared to the houses she'd lived in all her life, the house was small. However, since Dora didn't view this house as a permanent residence, she believed it would suit her needs. She probably wouldn't visit Fairfield more than three or four times each year. Both the cook and the maid who'd worked for the previous owner were pleased to remain in her employ and stay in the residence while she was in New York. Dora felt that she'd made a wise decision to own her own home.

To celebrate buying the house, Dora planned a dinner. She invited George Vanderbilt and his sister, as well as Allen and Timothy. As it turned out, she and Allen had the evening to themselves. Timothy absolutely refused to come, telling Allen that he'd feel like a "fish out of water."

"I can't even talk to Miss Porter when she's on the farm without stammering and stuttering, so I'd be miserable," Timothy argued. "Besides, I've never seen Mr. Vanderbilt or his sister. I just won't go. Will you explain it to her?"

Allen had become greatly attached to his younger brother, and he knew exactly how he felt. He wasn't looking forward to sitting down to eat with the Vanderbilts, either, but he wouldn't hurt Dora's feelings by refusing her invitation. He'd hurt her too many times when he wouldn't involve himself in her way of life.

As it turned out, George and his sister were called to New York for a family board meeting, so only Allen and Dora sat down to dinner. The table was long, one that would probably have seated ten or more guests quite comfortably, and the maids had put place settings at opposite ends of the table. After they were seated, Allen laughed, "I can hardly see you in this dim candlelight. I'm going to sit closer to you." He got up and moved to a chair beside her.

"Mattie is going to join us as soon as the maids have served us, so there will be three of us."

Allen had given some thought to what he should wear to the dinner and ended up choosing his best church clothes. Perhaps knowing that he wouldn't be wearing anything formal, Dora had donned one of the dresses she wore to the office. He was amazed sometimes at the effort she put forth to try to follow the lifestyle of the people who lived in Fairfield.

While they ate, Dora started explaining some of her ideas for the mill. Allen had hinted that the income of absentee landowners probably wasn't as lucrative as if the owner lived in the area where the business was located. Still, her father owned enterprises in several different locations, and he had prospered. If the system worked for him, why wouldn't it be profitable for her? She was confident she could persuade Allen to manage the mill for her. With him in charge, she wouldn't have any worries about the mill productivity.

On that point, Dora soon learned that she was mistaken.

"You've been such a help to me in understanding the importance of the mill and the best way to operate it. I'm depending on you to take care of my interests when I'm not here."

Allen shook his head and interrupted her with a lift of his right hand.

"I thought I'd already made it plain that I won't do that. If this mill belongs to you, it's *your* responsibility to manage it. Absentee landlords—or ladies, in your case—are rarely successful in operating a business. I won't accept the responsibility of property that belongs to someone else."

"But you know more about the mill and this part of the country than I do!"

"Of course! And how do you think I learned that? By living here for ten years. When I came to this area from South Carolina, I didn't know a textile mill from a sawmill or a mountain from a foothill. I'd always lived in flat land, but I settled down and learned to live the necessary way to succeed in this country. All kinds of things can happen in a textile mill that would require the owner's immediate attention. There could be a tragedy of some sort, and you might be in New York, or even in Europe. And no matter who you hire to work for you, no overseer will give a hundred percent to any project unless it's to his interest to do so."

"But you've told me what I should pay a manager," Dora said, obviously puzzled that anyone would turn down such a handsome offer.

"You asked me what it would cost to hire a good manager, and I answered it. I didn't tell you I considered it a good idea."

They finished their meal in silence. When Allen laid aside his napkin, he didn't know if he'd hurt Dora's feelings or if she was angry. "I don't suppose you'll believe me, but I'm sorry I can't do what you want me to. I'd like to please you, but I won't do so at your expense or at my discomfort."

Dora didn't comment, but her facial expression relaxed until he decided she wasn't angry at him. "Some people value independence, free will, and contentment more than money," he continued, "and I'm one of them. No doubt you can find many competent men who will jump at the chance to manage the cotton mill, but it won't be me."

"You're stubborn, aren't you?"

"That's not the term I would use," Allen said, smiling at her. "I believe *intelligent* or *independent* would be a better word. The trouble with you, Dora, is that all your life you've been accustomed to having your own way, and I'm just like you in that respect. I've become very fond of you, and I'd like to do what you ask, but I won't become responsible for the mill. I'm a carpenter and a farmer. If you want some construction done, I'll do it, but I won't work in a textile mill. Fairfield Textile Mill will soon belong to you. It's your responsibility, not mine. If you don't want it, sell it."

Dora's eyes snapped angrily. She drew a deep breath and swallowed awkwardly, obviously trying to control her tongue. At length she said quietly, "I've told you that Father has strings attached to it. If I sell the mill, he'll disinherit me."

Allen shrugged. "That might be the best gift he will ever give you."

It wasn't until Allen left that Dora realized he was suggesting she would be better off if she were disinherited. Was he thinking that if she were no longer heir to a fortune that they might have a future together? Although he hadn't given any verbal indication that he loved her, Dora had occasionally seen expressions in Allen's eyes that made her believe he was as attracted to her as she was to him. Sighing, she found it difficult to imagine that two people as different as she and Allen could ever have a future together. Why, of all the men she'd met in her life, had she developed an affinity for Allen Bolden?

Still angry with him, without even a good-bye, Dora left the next day for New York. She gave Allen her address, asking him to notify her if he thought she was needed at the mill. As always, Allen was a man of few words, and he didn't say if he would or wouldn't keep in touch with her.

Chapter 6

Dora reclined on an upholstered sofa on the eighth floor of the apartment building watching the activities in Central Park through a large window. Although physically she was in New York, her mind was centered on the small town of Fairfield and the textile mill she owned there, which she left two months ago. Today she'd received the deed that had transferred the textile mill to her.

True to his nature, her father had attached a "string" to the gift. If she didn't keep the property for ten years, ownership of the mill would revert to him. If she managed the property for ten years, it would belong to her. Regardless of whose name was on the deed, Dora knew her father would always intend to tell her how to manage the mill. If that was his plan, he was going to be in for a rude awakening. As soon as they affixed their signatures to the transfer of ownership, she was going to operate the mill as she wanted to. She had a feeling that he would soon regret the business transaction because she'd insisted on a clause in the deed giving her complete control of management for three years.

Dora loved her father—after all, he was the only family she had, except for some cousins—but she would not let him dominate her life any longer. When she was younger, they'd traveled together to far-flung nations of the world and had enjoyed wonderful companionship. It was only when she turned twenty-one, and by law was old enough to manage her own affairs, that he became dictatorial. Several times she'd been tempted to tell her father that she didn't want his money—that she valued her independence more than riches. She had inherited a sizable amount of money from her mother's family, over which he had no control, so even if her father disinherited her, she wouldn't be destitute. He hadn't been pleased when she refused to let him invest that money for her, and if she angered him too much, she wouldn't put it past him to disinherit her and leave his estate to a nephew, Blake Porter, a man Dora didn't like. She didn't need his wealth to survive, but she surely didn't want Blake to have it.

Since she'd left North Carolina, she hadn't heard anything from Allen, which both distressed and annoyed her. He was constantly in her thoughts during the day, and she dreamed about him almost every night. The dreams were hazy, and most of the time when she awakened, she couldn't remember the content of them. Was she in love with Allen Bolden? Dora had experienced minor love affairs since she was in her teens. Most of her admirers had been boys of her own age, but at one time, she'd imagined herself in love with their thirty-year-old butler.

To fancy herself in love with Allen was almost as far-fetched as her puppy love for the butler. They had nothing in common. Even if he loved her, she couldn't see any future for them. She couldn't imagine herself living in the mountains of North Carolina the rest of her life, and she knew that Allen's roots were planted too deeply in that area for him to live elsewhere. Certainly not in New York City!

Since she'd been home, her father had been hinting that it was time for her to get married, and he already had a prospective man in mind—a widower fifteen years older than she. Lester Holdredge was rich, of course, for her father wouldn't have considered a poor man, being the owner of a chain of hotels throughout the state, as well as other real estate. She had nothing against Lester. He was an honorable man who'd make anyone a good husband— anyone except her.

She ignored her father's overtures, wondering more than once if she would find happiness anywhere except with Allen. She'd considered telling her father that she didn't want his money, but there was a larger barrier between Allen and her than finances.

Dora knew he would never consider her for his wife when she didn't share his Christian faith. She remembered a comment he'd made about a couple who worked at the mill. The wife attended the same church Allen did, but the man spent most of his weekends, as well as his salary, in a local bar. While her mother-in-law supervised their children, the woman worked at the mill to feed her family. Allen had remarked that she should never have married the man in the first place because she knew his questionable habits. He'd quoted a verse to the effect that believers should not be unequally yoked with nonbelievers.

If Allen loved her, and she suspected that he did, he wouldn't ask her to marry him, not only because of the difference in their family background and wealth, but also because she didn't share his Christian faith. Rather than criticizing him for being stubborn, she was actually proud of him because he placed his convictions above all else.

After they'd returned to New York, she'd borrowed Maude's Bible. She didn't understand much of what she read, but with the woman's help, she'd found the verse that Allen had quoted. " 'Be ye not unequally yoked together with unbelievers.' "

When she'd asked Maude what that verse meant, the maid favored her with a surprised facial expression before answering, "I'm not a Bible scholar, miss, but I believe it means that people ought to marry somebody who has the same religion they have. My folks were both Methodists, and they got along fine. I'm not suggesting that other religions are wrong, mind you, but it works better for man and wife to believe the same."

"But what if one partner has no religion at all, and the other one is a committed Christian? Would they have a good marriage?"

"Those marriages sometimes turn out very well, but many dedicated believers won't marry an unbeliever."

Dora asked no more questions, but she'd been disgruntled the rest of the day. Why was she fretting over the situation anyway? There wasn't anything romantic between her and Allen, and she knew him well enough to wonder if there ever would be. Despite her feelings for him, she knew their backgrounds were too different for any future together. The thought made her irritable most of the time, and she had no interest in seeing anyone.

For instance, Lester Holdredge had been stopping by for visits. Lester and his wife, Matilda, had been friends of the family for several years, and

Lester had been footloose since Matilda had died the previous year. He was a retired schoolteacher, and Dora had encouraged him to do some substitute work just to pass the time, but he was still lonely. She felt sorry for the man, and since he lived in the same apartment building, he stopped by to see her almost every day. He had never proposed to her, but he had given several indications that he would be interested in marrying again, should the opportunity arise.

He had stopped by this morning for an unannounced visit, and he had been boring Dora for an hour as he discussed all of his achievements. She knew he wasn't exaggerating, but she'd heard all of it before. So if Lester thought she was impressed by his achievements and was about ready to propose, he was in for a rude awakening. While he talked, in her thoughts she compared him to Allen, knowing that Lester didn't have a chance for a positive answer to a proposal if he ever got up his nerve to ask her.

Allen had never trusted Ted Morgan, who'd been hired a few months before the sale of the mill and retained by Mr. Porter when Allen refused to become the new manager, although he didn't have a reason for his distrust. As far as Allen could tell, the man had performed his work adequately until the news arrived that ownership of the mill had passed to Dora. Morgan sent word to Allen that he had some carpentry work for him to do at the mill. Allen completed building a barn for his neighbor before he went to the textile mill to see what Morgan wanted.

He was curious and somewhat surprised when Morgan explained that he wanted Allen to build an office for him across the street from the mill. The manager had even drawn a sketch of how he wanted the building completed. To follow Morgan's plans would entail quite a sum of money, so after the man explained what he wanted done, Allen commented, "I assume that you've discussed this project with the owner and that she approves of the construction."

Morgan frowned. "I'm the manager of this mill. I make the decisions of what needs to be done."

With a shrug, Allen said, "You have that right, but I'm not building anything unless the owner tells me to."

"Then I'll get another carpenter," Morgan said angrily.

"Suits me," Allen said and walked out the door, thinking that the absentee owner had better put in an appearance, or Morgan would steal her blind.

Allen was a firm believer in not involving himself in other people's affairs. He'd made it plain to Dora that he wouldn't manage the business for her, but he knew she considered him a friend. Was it right for him to do nothing while Ted Morgan mishandled the textile mill's funds and stole her inheritance? Dora had asked him to notify her if anything went wrong, but he hadn't promised he would. Still, should he stand aside and watch the downfall of an industry that was the lifeline of Fairfield? He had not only Dora's interest at heart, but also concern for his friends and neighbors who would lose their livelihoods if the mill closed. He spent one whole evening writing a letter trying to explain to Dora what would probably happen to the mill if Morgan continued to manage it. He tore up several copies of the letter before he threw his pen aside. He wasn't any good at putting his thoughts on paper.

Since Dora had told him to contact her if she needed to return to Fairfield, he knew she should know what was going on. Without attempting to understand his decision, a few days later, leaving Timothy to look after the farm, Allen went into Asheville and bought new clothes and caught the local train to Richmond with New York City as his ultimate destination. Three days later when he arrived at Grand Central Station in New York, he sat on one of the benches in the station and gave serious consideration to his reason for coming. He was half tempted to catch a train back to North Carolina without letting Dora know he'd come to the city. Although she was friendly enough in Fairfield, she might be ashamed to have him show up at her New York apartment. Even with his new clothes—perhaps because of them—he still looked like a country hick, and he figured he'd be an embarrassment to her.

He bought a meal in one of the station's restaurants, amazed at the cost and wondering if his money would last until he returned to Fairfield. Fortunately, he'd bought a round-trip ticket. At a newspaper stand he inquired about the distance to Dora's apartment, gratified to learn that it was in walking distance.

When he reached the apartment building, he checked his suitcase with the doorman and took the elevator to the eighth floor. He stood outside her door for a few minutes before he had the courage to knock. For all he knew, she might be on a tour of Europe or traveling in the United States, and he would have made the trip for nothing. He heard footsteps approaching and didn't realize he was holding his breath until a woman he'd never seen opened the door. At first he thought he must have the wrong apartment, but noting that the woman wore a navy blue uniform, he assumed she was a servant.

"I'm looking for Dora Porter. Do I have the right apartment?"

The maid looked him over from head to toe before she said, "Do you have a calling card?"

Realizing more than ever that he was a fish out of water, Allen shook his head. He didn't even know what a calling card was.

"Just a moment, please."

The woman didn't invite him in and started to

close the door when he heard soft footsteps approaching and Dora's voice saying, "Who is it?"

She reached the door, and for a moment a stunned expression covered her face before she gave a tiny squeal, pushed past the maid, and threw her arms around him.

"Oh Allen," she said. "I've missed seeing you."

Momentarily speechless, Allen stood like a man turned to stone before his emotions surfaced and he drew her into a tight embrace.

"I almost turned back before I rang the bell," he murmured, "not knowing whether you'd want to see me, but it can't get much better than this. I believe you're happy to see me, so that's worth the long trip up here."

Allen glanced at the maid and almost laughed at her scandalized expression. She shrugged her shoulders and walked away.

"Oh Allen," Dora murmured. "I am happy to see you. Come on in. I'm not conceited enough to believe that you came all the way to New York just to see me, so I suppose there's trouble at the mill. Just let me get used to the fact that you're really here before you unload any bad news."

He knew now that he had missed her and *had* come to New York primarily to see Dora, although he couldn't admit it to her. He'd not wanted to love Dora, but there wasn't any doubt in his mind now that he did love her and that he'd made the long trip to see her more than to warn her about problems at the mill. He could have sent that warning by letter. Why was he so foolish to love a woman who was as far out of his reach as the sun and the moon? Well, he was here now, so he might as well enjoy a taste of paradise for a few days.

With her arm around his waist, Dora led Allen into the living room, where Lester Holdredge was still sitting. She'd forgotten all about the man, and she wondered how she could explain his presence to Allen and vice versa. From where he sat, Lester could have seen her embrace Allen.

She felt her face flushing and, fearful that she had a guilty look, she took Allen's hand and drew him into the room. "Let me introduce you to Lester Holdredge, a friend of the family. Lester, this is my friend, Allen Bolden, who is looking after the affairs of the family's textile mill in North Carolina."

"I can come back later," Allen said.

"Oh no," Dora said.

Standing, Lester shook hands with Allen. "That isn't necessary. I was just preparing to leave."

Dora walked to the door with him, trying not to show how eager she was for him to leave. Why had Allen come to New York? Whatever the reason, she was delighted to see him.

* * *

Allen stood at the wide window overlooking the park, Dora at his side. He'd always known that his world and Dora's were eons apart, but if he'd needed more proof, the location of this apartment made it evident. Even in the mountains, he'd heard of Central Park and the expensive dwellings and businesses around the area.

He heard footsteps behind them, and Dora turned. Maude had entered the room with a tray and greeted Allen graciously before she set several items on a long table in front of the davenport. "It's good to have you visit, Mr. Bolden. Do you want me to pour?"

"No thanks," Dora said. "I'll take care of it."

"Ring if you need anything else."

Dora sat on the davenport and invited Allen to sit with her.

"I'm not hungry," he said. "I ate at the train station."

"Regardless, you can drink another cup of coffee or tea and eat a cinnamon roll while you tell me why you're here. As I said, you couldn't have made the trip just to see *me*. Is there something wrong at the mill?"

Allen smiled. "As far as I know, everything inside the mill is all right. It's Ted Morgan. Maybe I just have a suspicious mind, but your manager is building himself an office. He's also driving a new buggy pulled by a team of thoroughbred horses, which I have an idea he bought with your money. If you approve of that, all right, but I'm sure your father wouldn't."

"It's your fault," she said, a stubborn expression on her face. It amused him to some extent—they hadn't been together fifteen minutes, and already they were disagreeing.

"My fault!" he said.

"Yes, your fault!" she answered. "If you'd taken over management of the mill as I wanted you to, there wouldn't have been any problem."

"If you'd move to North Carolina like you ought to," he retorted, "there wouldn't be any trouble. With your intelligence and your riches, you could make that textile mill one of the best in the whole country."

"You still don't understand, do you?" She stood and walked to the window again. With a sweep of her hand, she asked, "After you've seen all of this, can't you realize what I'd be giving up to move to North Carolina?"

"Of course I can," Allen said and followed her to the window. His legs were still stiff from sitting for hours on the long train ride, and he wanted to stand.

"You'd be leaving the noise, smoke, and crowded streets where people don't even look at each other as they're hurrying from one place to the other. If you'd leave this behind, you'd be gaining a view of the mountains, fresh air, and the opportunity to turn the Fairfield Textile Mill into a business that would not only be profitable for your employees, but also to you. You'd have neighbors and friends who would have your best interest at heart and would help you in any way necessary."

Dora sniffed. "And I suppose you think that would compensate for giving up the lifestyle I've had since childhood. It doesn't matter to me whether I inherit his fortune or not. My grandmother left me plenty of money, but I don't want Father to give his wealth to a cousin I don't even like."

"I believe your father is testing you. It's your choice, of course, and if you want to continue to be an absentee landlord, so be it. I thought it was only right for me to warn you that, if the present trend continues, Ted Morgan will probably steal you blind and maybe ruin the business in the process. I normally don't meddle in other people's affairs, but you're my friend, and I couldn't get it out of my mind to tell you. I've done that now, so I'll head back to North Carolina."

He turned toward the door, and she jerked on his coattail.

"You'll do no such thing," she said, an annoyed expression on her face. "When I've missed you for weeks, the least you can do is stay a day or two. At least stay long enough to see some of New York so you will realize how my life would change if I commit to spending the rest of my life in North Carolina.

And if you've come bearing any more bad news, wait until you're ready to go home to tell me."

"I'll stay one night," Allen agreed. "Then I'll head south. I can't afford to stay in this city very long."

"If you'll be reasonable, it won't cost you anything except your train fare. We have an apartment on the floor below, which Father keeps for visiting business associates. You can stay there free of charge, and I'd like for you to take your meals with me. It's lonely eating alone. Consider it a return for all the things you did for me when I was in North Carolina."

"All right, I'll accept your hospitality for one night. Now I want to know what you plan to do with the mill. It's none of my business, but you asked me to alert you to any problems. Morgan is a problem."

"What is he doing or not doing? Do you think he'll steal from me?"

"Now, Dora, you know me well enough to realize that I won't speculate on what *might* happen. At this point, I don't know that Morgan is dishonest, but he is greedy. I suspect he's purchasing things, like that new buggy, for his own benefit. He may have paid for the buggy with his own money, but I doubt it."

"I certainly didn't authorize a new buggy for him."

"I could be wrong, but someone hinted to me that he used company money to buy it. He's also sped up production, and since he's being paid a percentage of the mill's income, he's increased the workload of the mill hands to make more money. They were already working long hours, and they're mad about it. Besides that, he's slow in authorizing necessary repairs to the company houses. For instance, part of the roof blew off the house where Kitty lives. He hasn't ordered a repair order yet."

"Isn't that the little crippled girl?"

Allen nodded.

"She's been on my mind a lot. Father has a good friend who's a surgeon here in the city. I'm sure he could easily repair the damage in her leg. I'd pay for it."

He nodded in agreement. "That's the type of thing you *should* do for your workers and their families. Their homes need repair, and most of the managers haven't been in any hurry to order the work done. It would be easy for you to sit here in luxury and not have any idea of the needs of your employees. My conscience wouldn't let me rest until you knew what the situation is, so rather than writing a letter, I decided to notify you personally. But I've meddled all I intend to. I've told you about the situation—that's all I can do. You'll have to take it from here. I may be wrong, but I still believe that if you continue to leave everything in Morgan's control, he'll bankrupt you."

"I wouldn't like that," Dora agreed. "And I can

already hear my father's reaction. I can't make decisions about the mill on the spur of the moment, though. If you're going to leave tomorrow, let's take a look at New York this afternoon. We'll hire a carriage."

Chapter 7

After they'd traveled through the palatial districts of the city, which Allen admitted were quite impressive, he said to the driver, "Buddy, let's take a look at the other face of New York. How about going down to the waterfront and to the ghettos? I've read the photo documentary *How the Other Half Lives* published by Jacob Riis. I'd like to see if his facts were true."

"I don't own this rig, and I ain't allowed to go certain places that you probably want to see," the driver said. "But I can take you to some areas where you'll get your eyes full."

Thanks to the driver, Allen had a tour of part of

the sprawling city of New York. After an hour, he
had seen enough to know that the reports he'd heard
of the pressures caused by industrialization, sprawling urban cities, violent labor uprisings, economic
depression, and fears of the middle classes in the cities were all true. He'd also witnessed firsthand the
difference between his upbringing and Dora's—seen
enough to realize that if he'd ever harbored dreams
that he and Dora could share a life, it was a false
hope. He noticed more than one building that had
the name Porter on it, and it was beyond his com-
prehension to understand how any one man could
have so much money.

Allen noticed that Dora had become quieter, but
he couldn't interpret the expression on her face as
they spent the next two hours visiting parts of New
York she probably hadn't seen before. Perhaps it was
time he came to New York so she would realize how
common people lived.

During the time he'd known her in North Carolina, Dora had given some strong indications that she
considered him more than a friend. She had hinted
that she would like to make him a partner in the
business, but when he ignored the hint, she hadn't
persisted. He'd thought at first that she might have
some interest in George Vanderbilt, but she'd only
been to Biltmore a few times and that was always
when he'd invited a group of people. And although
he admitted that he wasn't any authority on the

working of a woman's mind, there were times when he thought that her hand on his shoulder seemed more of a caress than a gentle touch.

Although he believed he hadn't harbored any hope that they could become a couple, he knew that he'd had his dreams, too. Dreams that, he now understood, could never come to fruition. He was sorry that he'd come to New York City, for the trip had only emphasized what he'd known all along. There was no future for him and Dora.

When they returned to her apartment, she said, "I'd like to take you to a Broadway play tonight, if you'll agree to go."

Allen couldn't think of anything he wanted to do less, but remembering that Dora entered without criticism into the slight entertainment around Fairfield, he agreed to go. To his surprise, he was captivated by the performance. Before they left her apartment, Dora had spent an hour telling him the story of the show they would see. He found it quite difficult to interpret the British pronunciation, but in spite of that, it was easy for him to follow the actors' performance, which followed the summary he'd read in advance.

An Ideal Husband *opens during a dinner party at the home of Sir Robert Chiltern in London, a respected member of the House of Commons. Sir Robert is being blackmailed by Mrs.*

Cheveley, who has been an enemy of Sir Robert's wife, Mabel, since their school days. Much of the conflict revolves around the stocks Sir Robert had bought in the construction of the Suez Canal before the British government announced its purchase. With this information Mrs. Cheveley attempts to blackmail Sir Robert to support a fraudulent scheme to build a canal in Argentina.

Lady Chiltern isn't aware of her husband's problems. Their marriage had been predicated on her having an "ideal husband." She isn't aware that Sir Robert had gathered his fortune through illicit means. Lord Goring urges Sir Robert to fight Mrs. Cheveley and reveal his guilt to his wife.

With many twists and turns the drama finally ended, leaving Allen confused and wondering why anyone would enjoy living in a city like this. He had at first refused to come to the theater with her, protesting that his new garments might be suitable for North Carolina but not New York. She said it wouldn't matter, but Allen was miserable knowing that he stuck out like a sore thumb with a brown tweed suit when the other men were dressed in black tuxedos and white shirts. He wouldn't have known the difference if she'd just taken him to a small theater, but he could tell when he entered that she'd taken him to one of the fanciest theaters in New York. When he not only looked like but thought like a country bumpkin, he asked Dora if he could sneak out a back door.

"Absolutely not," she said. He grew even more surprised when Dora introduced him to dozens of her acquaintances as her friend from North Carolina. He'd believed that he couldn't possibly think of Dora more highly than he already did, but if she was ashamed of his appearance, he couldn't tell it. She didn't treat him any differently in Haymarket Theater than she did when they walked the streets of Fairfield.

Allen's train didn't leave until noon the next day, so he and Dora enjoyed a leisurely breakfast and took a walk in Central Park before he left. While they walked, Dora took his hand. He squeezed it gently as they walked down the tree-lined paths, and Allen enjoyed the beauty of the area. When they walked through slightly wooded areas, he was reminded of some of the forest areas near Fairfield, especially the area where he'd met Dora. How much his life had changed since then! He had never doubted that he would live out his days on earth as a bachelor. After all, he'd lived unmarried more than thirty years, and it never entered his mind that he'd meet somebody like Dora and it would be "love at first sight." Although he would never ask her to marry him, he was convinced that he did love her.

"I wish you didn't have to leave so soon," Dora complained as they approached her apartment. "When will I see you again?"

He raised his eyebrows. "That's up to you. I can't afford a trip to New York City very often. If you want to see me, you know where to find me."

Maude served sandwiches and hot tea to them when they returned to the apartment. Allen complimented her on the pastries, and she seemed pleased. It was obvious that she approved of him.

"But you will let me know if you think I need to come to Fairfield?" Dora insisted.

He frowned. "I came all the way to New York to notify you that an absentee owner is not a good idea, especially in this case. I've told you several times that you need to oversee the textile mill yourself—not pay someone else to do it. Unless I'm called to do some carpentry work, I don't have any reason to be in the textile mill, so it isn't likely I'll know what Morgan is doing. I'm not going to be your spy. Since my brother has come to live with me, I'm staying on the farm every night—not stopping over at Aunt Sallie's Boardinghouse sometimes when I'm working beyond Fairfield. I've warned you what is happening, and that's all I can do. I can't make decisions for you."

Pulling his watch from his pocket, Allen said, "I have to leave."

"I wish you would stay another day or two, but if I can't convince you, I'll go to the station with you. That will give us a little more time. It's hard to tell when we'll be together again." They put on their coats, but at the door Dora tugged on his sleeve. Tears came into her eyes, and she leaned against him. Was this an act to get him to stay a few more days, or would she really miss him? He'd enjoyed this short visit with her so much that he knew how lonely he'd be when he returned to Asheville. If he ever doubted that he loved Dora, this visit had made him realize that love had come to him at last. Why did he have to fall in love with a woman he couldn't have? There were too many differences in their backgrounds and way of life for him to ever entertain a closer relationship. His mind was telling him that, but his heart had another message.

He dropped the suitcase to the floor and pulled her toward him. With a surprised glance, she snuggled into his arms and placed her head on his shoulder. He felt her rapid heartbeat, and if he'd ever doubted that she really did care for him, he would never doubt it again.

Frustrated at the futility of their relationship, Allen held Dora close for a short time. When she lifted her tear-stained face, he lowered his lips to hers. There was no way he could ever have her, so why couldn't he stop involving himself in her business? Would it be possible for him to return to North Carolina and ever be content again? Before Dora came to Asheville, he'd been happy with his lifestyle, having no other thought except to live in happy bachelorhood. Now the prospect of living out his life as a single man left him feeling empty and distressed. A long future of dissatisfaction loomed before him.

When he released her, she said, "I don't know which is the hardest—not seeing you at all or to have you to myself for two whole days then having to say good-bye again. Do you know that I sometimes wish I'd never come to Fairfield in the first place?"

He smiled slightly. "I know what you mean. Both of us might have been happier if we'd never seen each other."

They were mostly silent as they walked toward the station.

"Will you write?" she asked after he'd checked the train schedule and found he had a half hour to wait.

"Write about what? The textile mill?"

"About anything you want to. I'll be interested in everything you do—how your farming venture turns out and if your brother stays with you or starts wandering again."

"I hope he stays. He seems to like the farm, and

he is a big help to me. Besides, I think he's sweet on Kitty."

"You mean the child who has the twisted leg."

"That's the one, but she really isn't a child. She's small for her age, but she's sixteen, an age when many of our girls get married."

"I'd like to help her. Father has a doctor friend who's a bone surgeon, and I feel sure he could mend her leg if she lived closer."

"The family wouldn't have the money to pay a surgeon even if he came to North Carolina."

"Oh, he does lots of charity work. If not, I'd pay for the surgery. It wouldn't cost her family anything."

"The local people like to consider themselves independent, and they're touchy about accepting handouts."

"Nevertheless, I'll give it some thought. I could ask the doctor to charge them a small amount to avoid any embarrassment."

Dora was silent the rest of their walk, and her face took on an expression that reminded him very much of her father. Allen knew that she was considering options, and she'd probably come up with some solution.

They sat on a bench in the corner to wait for the southbound train to arrive. Since they'd said their good-byes at the apartment, Allen prepared to leave when the train rumbled into the station. There didn't seem anything else to do or say. Dora's eyes glistened with unshed tears, and he squeezed the hand she held out to him and bent over for one last kiss. Dora knew her father would have a fit if he ever heard she'd been kissed in the nonprivacy of a large train station, but at that moment, she didn't care if President Cleveland himself witnessed the kiss. She sniffed and tried to stop crying as Allen boarded the train, but she stood close to the train and waited until he found a seat in a forward car and waved to her. She stood watching until the train left the station, her face covered in tears. If he lived to be a hundred years old, Allen knew he'd never forget this moment. There was no doubt that she really did love him. Was he foolish to reject the love she was so eager to share with him?

Chapter 8

Dora watched for the mail every day, not expecting Allen to write but hoping that he would. She was determined not to be the first one to make contact, but after a few months she missed him so much that she decided to do something about it. She bought a thinking-of-you card. It was a rural setting, which reminded her of North Carolina. The ground was covered with snow, and a red barn was featured in the background. The message read, *"To wish you health and happiness."* As Dora prepared the card to mail it, she wondered if she was making a mistake. She almost wished that she could change the word *health* to *wealth*, for she was convinced that her wealth and his lack of it was what kept Allen from seeking a closer relationship with her. She wrote a note on the card wishing him well for the coming year.

To her surprise, he answered her note. He misspelled a few words, which made her wonder if his lack of education as well as his few worldly possessions kept him from declaring his love for her. Frustrated because of the seeming impossibility of any serious relationship between them, Dora slept with the letter under her pillow for a week. When she received the annual report of the financial status of the Fairfield Textile Mill, she was amazed to find that instead of making a profit, the mill had actually lost money. She also noted the annual bonus gift to the workers had not been paid. Why hadn't she listened to Allen?

She knew that her father would hear about it because, until she proved that she could operate the mill, he was to receive copies of the same financial reports she did. Two days later he stormed into the apartment, waving the mill report. It was a stormy session, which ended when he said, "Missy, you have another six months to put the business on a paying status, or I'm taking control."

Six months ago she would have shouted at him and told him to keep the mill. Instead, she said, "Very well! Six months it is, but during that time, I won't tolerate any interference from you. I can't make decisions if I feel as if you're looking over my shoulder all the time. I didn't want that mill, but you forced it upon me. If I've made a failure of operating the business, it's your fault as well as mine. However, I'm going back to Asheville to prove to you that I have as much business acumen as you have. If at the end of a year, I haven't made a success of the business, I'll return it to you gladly."

To her surprise, he agreed not to interfere, and Dora started making plans to move to North Carolina. Maude agreed to go with her, but not wanting to burn all of her bridges behind her, Dora sublet the apartment to a cousin who wanted to move to the city. If she couldn't make a profit on the mill, she would have a home to return to.

She debated a long time wondering if she should notify Allen and Ted Morgan that she was returning. She finally decided she would have a better opportunity to catch Morgan in his theft if no one knew she was coming. Maude wasn't happy about moving away from New York, but she'd been Dora's companion for years and neither one of them knew what she'd do without the other.

So when she and Maude stepped off the train in Fairfield in October, her arrival was unexpected. She left Maude at the train station with the luggage and walked down the street toward the textile mill. Several people saw her and gave her friendly greetings, but she didn't stop to talk to anyone until she met Allen coming out of the post office.

The expression of surprise, as well as pleasure, on his face encouraged her, and she believed that she had made the right decision to plant her roots in North Carolina. As unlikely as it seemed, she believed that she would never be completely happy unless this man was her husband. The few letters she'd had from him had left her dissatisfied with the separation. Allen might not fall in love with her even if she lived in North Carolina, but it was a sure thing that marriage between them wouldn't be possible if she stayed in New York. At that moment she wasn't sorry she'd burned her bridges behind her, and she hoped that she never would be.

Speechless, Allen stared at her until she stepped closer and put her hand on his arm. "I'm not a ghost, my dear." In spite of his surprise, his eyes glowed with affection. Hope swelled inside her that he wasn't indifferent about seeing her.

"I don't know what to say. Why didn't you let me know you were coming?"

"I didn't want anyone in Fairfield to know I was coming, especially Ted Morgan. Maude is with me, as well as two accountants to check the business records of the mill. We just got off the train, and I came here first of all to confront Morgan so he couldn't destroy any records. Will you go into his office with me? It won't be a pleasant encounter."

"Sure, I'll go." He stepped up on the small porch, opened the door for her, then stood aside as Dora entered. He stayed in the small lobby when she walked toward the luxurious office Morgan had created.

The door was open, and a man sat behind a desk. Massively built, but muscular rather than fat, the man had a strong face and bushy brows that jutted over his dark eyes. Dora assumed that he was the mill's business manager. With a slight knock on the door, she caught his attention and entered the room.

"Mr. Morgan?" she questioned.

He stood. "Yes, ma'am. How can I help you?"

She opened the briefcase she carried and removed several papers, which she laid on the desk. "These papers will identify me. I'm Dora Porter, owner of the Fairfield Textile Mill. After the past six months brought no income whatever to me, I decided it wasn't good to be an absentee owner. I'm moving to North Carolina and, starting today, I'll assume my duties as the mill owner. Those documents deal with your dismissal as business manager here, effective immediately. There's also a court order prohibiting you from removing anything from this office until the auditors have made a thorough investigation."

"What auditors?" he snarled.

"I brought two of the best qualified auditors in New York City with me. They're going to examine the mill's books. One of them will stay here in the office at all times until this examination is completed. I haven't been pleased with the low income from the mill during the past few months."

"Then you don't trust me?" His black eyes blazed with hatred and some other emotion. Was it guilt or fear?

"I don't know if I *can* trust you, but I'll give you the benefit of the doubt until the audit is completed. Regardless, as of today, I'm taking over management of the mill, and if I'm mistaken in my suspicions, I'll give you a recommendation elsewhere."

"I don't need your help to find a job," he said as he jerked his coat off a hall tree. He locked the door to an adjacent room. "That's my bedroom and living room combined. Nothing in there belongs to you, so stay out of it."

"I'll give you a week to remove your possessions. After that, I'll open the room and store the contents."

He passed Dora without another look, but stopped when he saw Allen in the other room. "I suppose you had something to do with this?"

Allen shrugged and lifted his arms in a negative gesture.

Dora stepped to the door, noting that the auditors she'd hired were also in the room. To Morgan, she said, "Allen didn't know I was coming to North Carolina until I met him in front of the post office, so don't blame him for your dismissal. These men are the New York auditors who found multiple errors in the records you sent to me. When all of these so-called mistakes always seemed to be in your favor, they insisted I should make some management changes."

One of the men, who'd been her father's partner in one of his enterprises for years, said, "One of us will stay here in the office all the time just to be sure the records aren't destroyed or…"

Storming out of the building without waiting for the auditor to finish, Morgan slammed the door behind him. She knew she'd made a bitter enemy, another incident to cause her trouble, but what else could she have done?

Dora introduced Allen to the two strangers, saying, "He's really been a friend and help to me. You won't mind if they ask you questions, will you?"

Allen shrugged his shapely shoulders. "But I may not have all the answers. I don't know anything about operating a textile mill. Since I'm my own boss, my schedule is flexible, and I'll help any way I can." Turning to the auditors, he said, "My first advice is that, for the time being, someone should be in this office building at all times. There's a comfortable bedroom behind the office. If you both need to be away and want me to stay here, let me know. But I know nothing about the mill's financial records, so I can't help with that."

"Actually," one of the auditors said, "we don't expect to find many records or, at best, they won't be complete. Dora says she doesn't intend to press charges against Morgan but, depending on the size of the embezzlement, she may demand that he make restitution. He surely has some of the money stashed away."

When the auditors left the building to move into the hotel for a few days, Allen turned to Dora. "I'd suggest that you have extra guards at the textile mill at all times, too, for a few weeks. At least until Morgan leaves town or makes a move of some kind."

"Do you think he would really have the nerve to sabotage the mill?"

"I have no idea," Allen said. "I'd never met the man until he came here to work."

"I asked you this before and you turned me down, but will *you* come to work for me? I want to be a success, I suppose to prove to Father that I'm not a spoiled debutante, but I can't do it without lots of help and advice."

He smiled and spoke gently. "The last time I refused to work for you was when you intended to stay in New York and only make occasional visits to Fairfield. Your intention to come here to live convinces me that you're serious about the success of the mill. I'll work for you. My brother has decided he wants to stay in North Carolina, and he can take care of the farm. Together we can turn this business into the best textile mill in North Carolina."

Chapter 9

Dora didn't delay her plans to revitalize the local textile mill. Taking Allen with her and Maude as a chaperone, she visited a few successful textile mills in South Carolina. They spent two days touring one mill and asking for advice. Not only did they visit the mill owners, but also the families who worked for them. Since Allen was more knowledgable than she, Dora mostly listened and took notes as he interviewed owners and workers alike.

They visited the home of one textile worker and talked to his wife, whose advice Dora considered invaluable. "My husband worked at a mill farther south for a few years," the woman explained. "But he likes it much better in this town, and so do I. There are good company stores, and sometimes when work is slack, the owner will give us food rather than require us to run a charge account. We can buy coal for six dollars a ton, although it's a few dollars more than that in other areas. Each miner's family has a garden where we can grow our own vegetables, too."

When Dora complimented the mill owner on his philanthropy, he smiled and said, "I'm not as noble as you think. It's a good business investment to ensure the comfort and goodwill of our workers. Sick and/or disgruntled workers are not going to give their best efforts. So I recommend this as a good policy to follow. The happier the workers are, the more money I make."

At another mill, they learned that the owner looked after his employees and their families as if they were members of one big family. He provided small but neat houses, some with lawns decorated with flowers. This owner also had a large farm and made available to the mill workers and their families milk, eggs, chickens, and vegetables at a reasonable price.

Dora didn't waste any time putting into practice the information they'd learned. She provided paint and wallpaper for each of the tenant houses. She rented Allen's farmland where Timothy and other men and women tended vegetable gardens, which the textile workers could buy at a reasonable price.

Within six months, she'd turned the town of Fairfield into the "Textile Mill Miracle Village," as it was touted in the local newspaper. Dora framed a portion of the article and hung it in the mill office to keep her reminded of her responsibilities to her employees.

> *Thanks to the proprietor of the local textile mill, Fairfield is being recognized near and far for its high quality of cotton fabric. If the employees in their spare time will do the labor, Miss Porter has also provided monetary help for the improvement of the company houses. The plant itself has undergone a renovation. More ceiling fans to remove the fabric lint away from the workers have been installed, and the mill is closed two Saturdays each month to allow employees more leisure time with their families. In spite of this, or perhaps because of it, the output of the plant has exceeded all expectations.*

Allen and Dora realized that the reason for the increase in production was because the workers were content and enjoyed their work. Dora had drawn heavily on the inheritance from her maternal grandmother for these improvements, which disturbed Allen. He advised her that the textile industry could decline and she might lose her capital, but he admitted Dora knew more about investment than he would ever know, so he didn't try to persuade her from her decision. Allen faithfully worked alongside her, helping in every way he could.

One afternoon when they were alone in the office, Dora had been checking the mill's increase in sales during the past six months. Allen was preparing the weekly salaries for the workers when Dora interrupted him. "I've got an idea."

Allen laughed and looked at her fondly, laying his pencil aside. "What now, bright eyes? I wish I had fifty dollars for every time you've made that statement since I've known you."

She held up a flyer that had come in the morning's mail. "This flyer concerns a traveling carnival that will be coming through the southern states this summer. Since the mill has exceeded all previous records for fabric output in the last six months, let's declare a holiday and arrange for the carnival to come to Fairfield."

"Sure. Are you going to take care of the financial arrangements?"

"For their own good, the workers need to learn to economize rather than spend all their money as soon as they receive it. Our mill's salaries are as high as any other mill in the South, so wouldn't it be fair enough to give them a day off with pay, then they could pay their own way?"

"Absolutely! We don't want them to take your

generosity for granted and start slacking in their work."

"Here's what the flyer says about the show. There will be a Ferris wheel, merry-go-round, and a few other smaller rides. Lots of places to buy cotton candy and other treats. It's not a very large carnival, but certainly enough to interest our people."

Always willing to listen to Dora, Allen leaned back in his chair. "Sounds like a good idea to me."

Within a week, Dora received a response from the carnival owner, who said they would be making a tour of North and South Carolina in two weeks and would enjoy spending a day and night at Asheville.

When she saw how happy the mill workers and their families were to have an opportunity for this recreation, Dora knew she'd made a wise choice. And not only mill workers but hundreds of people from the surrounding region converged on Asheville when the carnival arrived. Not wanting to leave the millsite without some supervision, Allen asked Timothy to stay in the office during the day while he went to the carnival, and he would stay in the evening.

Allen and Dora went to the carnival together. Allen had only intended to be a sightseer, but Dora persuaded him to ride the Ferris wheel and merry-go-round with her. His life hadn't allowed much time for recreation and he hadn't intended to go, but Dora had persuaded him. He felt pretty stupid straddling a horse on the merry-go-round, but when lots of other adults were riding, he didn't feel out of place. More and more, he found himself agreeing to do what Dora wanted, except in one very important situation. He couldn't actually believe that Dora would marry him, although at times he wondered.

During the time Dora was engrossed in improving living and work conditions in Fairfield, her father was on an extended business tour of Europe. When he came home and learned that Dora had spent most of her grandmother's inheritance, he was so angry that his friends actually feared he would have a stroke or heart attack. Maude's sister passed the word on, so Dora wasn't surprised one day when he stormed into the mill office and confronted her. As he ranted and raved about what she'd done, Dora actually feared for his life. His face was red, his eyes piercing, and he was shaking as though he had the ague.

"What have you done! What *have* you done! To think that a daughter of mine would spend a fortune on a run-down textile mill. If you'd invested in some of the ventures I suggested to you, you'd have made a lot more money."

His words annoyed Dora so much that she clutched a bolt of cotton cloth in her hand, using all of her willpower not to throw it at her father. Drawing a deep breath, she tried to speak calmly. "It was *you* who bought this 'run-down textile mill' and foisted it on me. If you remember, I didn't want the mill in the first place."

"You shouldn't have made all the improvements you did. You could have made just as much money by keeping the old equipment. I can't believe that a child of mine would waste her inheritance in such a manner!"

Dora grew tired of his recriminations. "Grandmamma willed all of her money to me, so I could use it for what I wanted. She didn't want me to be completely dependent on you, and she knew very well that if you got your hands on that money, I wouldn't have a dime to call my own."

"You've wasted the money."

"That's a matter of opinion. We disagree on that just as we do everything else. I used the money to improve conditions at the mill. It's recognized now as one of the best-managed mills in the South."

He snorted angrily. Dora looked helplessly at Allen, and he said, "Mr. Porter, why don't you take a look at the mill as it is now before you pass judgment on what has been wasted?"

"You keep out of this, Bolden. I have a feeling that you've been instrumental in her decisions."

"Think what you will, but that isn't true," Allen said calmly. "I've only made suggestions when Dora asked for them. Actually, I'd be happy to take credit for the improvements she's made. There's no other textile mill like it in the country. The workers are happy, and contented employees produce more revenue than disgruntled ones. The mill's output has increased steadily over the past few months. We have people all over the Carolinas applying for jobs here. Experienced businessmen congratulate Dora on the quality of the textiles."

Laughing, Oliver ignored the plus results and replied, "Why wouldn't the workers be happy? They're treated like kings. I couldn't believe that you'd actually renovated every dwelling, giving this town the reputation of being the 'gem of company houses.' What are you going to do when you need more repairs? What if you have to replace equipment when your money is all gone?"

"I carry insurance on the workers and buildings in such event. Besides, satisfied workers are careful workers, and now that they have reliable looms to work with, we seldom have any breakdowns."

Paying no attention to what Allen said, her father continued his tirade until Allen couldn't stand it any longer. He prayed silently, asking God to control his temper. Standing, he walked to the door.

"Mr. Porter, I won't stand aside and listen to you shout at Dora. This is not your property, so either control your temper or get out. If you don't go willingly, I'll put you out."

"It's not your property either. What right do you have to tell me how to deal with my daughter? I suppose you intend to gain control of the mill by forcing your attentions on her. I've heard that you came to New York to see her." Smirking at Dora, he said, "You didn't think I'd find that out, did you?"

"I should have known you'd have spies watching me, but I didn't make any secret that Allen was visiting me. What's happened that you've turned into such a bitter man? Have you ever considered how Mother would feel if she knew the way you are today? Please go back to New York, and stop meddling in my business." Allen walked to the door and motioned for the man to leave.

"I don't have to be ordered out twice. I'm through with you—you're no longer a daughter of mine." Swearing, he gave Allen a shove as he left the office.

The woebegone look on Dora's face pierced Allen to the quick, and he went to her quickly and drew her into a tight embrace. "Dearest, he didn't mean all of those things. I don't know what's wrong with the man. Perhaps he's mentally ill."

Dora put her arms around Allen's waist and sobbed. She was trembling all over, and he was so angry he prayed silently for God to forgive his negative thoughts about Mr. Porter.

"Right now I'm so unhappy—disillusioned or something—that I don't want to do anything. I don't care what happens to the mill. I suppose it boils down to the fact that I just want someone to love me.

I can't remember a mother's love, and obviously my father doesn't love me."

Allen held her tenderly. "I know I shouldn't tell you this because I don't intend to pursue anything serious between us. But I've been in love with you since the day George Vanderbilt threw the big party at Biltmore and you and I spent most of the day together. And in a different sense, your employees love you. You're loved more than you know."

Sniffing, she picked up on the words he hadn't intended to say. "Why *can't* there be anything between us? If Father carries out his threat to disinherit me and if I'm a failure at operating the textile mill, in a few years you'll probably have more money than I do."

He shook his head. "In the first place, I don't think your father is going to disinherit you. He's just trying to force your hand. He reminds me of a ten-year-old kid who throws a tantrum when he can't have his way. If you just ignore him and don't give in to his bullying, he'll eventually simmer down and act like a mature human being should. In addition to that, I'm going to see to it that you're successful as the only woman I know who owns and operates a textile mill. That is, if that's what you want to do."

"Let me think about it overnight. My mind is too muddled now to make any serious decisions."

He kissed her lightly on the lips before he released

her. "I'm going out to the farm now to see that all is well with Timothy, then I'm returning to spend the night here in the office. Try to get a good night's sleep, and we'll deal with the future tomorrow."

He kissed her forehead, walked with her to the door, and locked it behind them.

The next day he went home as soon it was daylight, helped Timothy with the chores, and prepared for church. When he walked into the sanctuary, he was amazed to see Dora and Maude seated with Aunt Sallie, the owner of the boardinghouse.

When Dora scooted over in the seat, he took that as an invitation to sit beside her, and with pleasure he joined her. Although Dora had indicated that she'd never attended church, she must have been able to read music because as they shared the same hymnbook, he noticed that she followed the notes easily. During the pastor's prayer prior to the sermon, Allen prayed without ceasing that God would send enlightenment in this morning's service to Dora so that she might be convicted of her need to be a follower of the Lord. He could hear Maude quietly praying, and although her words were muted, he was convinced that she was also concerned about Dora's lack of faith.

It seemed to Allen that the invitation hymn was meant completely for Dora. She started to sing, but when they reached the chorus, she closed her hymnal and bowed her head.

He prayed that the words of the chorus spoke to her heart.

"Speak Thou in softest whispers, whispers of
    love to me;
Thou shalt be always conqu'ror, Thou shalt
    be always free.
Speak Thou to me each day, Lord, always in
    tend'rest tone,
Let me now hear Thy whisper, 'Thou art not
    left alone.' "

At the conclusion of the service as the worshippers greeted each other, Allen couldn't read Dora's expression, so he didn't know if he was mistaken in his belief that she had been touched by the message. Aunt Sallie had to return to her boardinghouse after the morning service, but Allen invited Maude and Dora to be his guests for lunch. He hired a carriage to take them into Asheville where they ate dinner at the Carolina Hotel. After he left them at Dora's home, he returned to the farm, somewhat puzzled about her. She had been moody during lunch and seemed lost in her own thoughts. He and Maude did most of the talking.

To his surprise, Allen had learned that Timothy was a good cook, and the boy sheepishly admitted that he'd worked at a restaurant in Columbia for several weeks. While he prepared their evening meal, Allen walked around the borders of his farm checking on the fences to be sure none of his few cattle had strayed into the workers' gardens. When he returned to the house, he was startled to see Dora and Maude waiting on the porch. Dora had obviously been crying, and he'd never seen such a woebegone expression on her beautiful face. He sat on the swing beside her and put his arm around her while she leaned on his shoulder and sobbed. Puzzled and alarmed, he turned to Maude.

"She's upset about the pastor's message this morning," Maude said. "I think she's under conviction, but she doesn't know what that means. She hasn't been in a church service since she was a child."

Although Allen had counseled with many people about their faith, he'd never sensed the need to choose the right words for divine guidance than he did at this moment. He didn't quote any scripture because he knew that Dora wouldn't understand, but praying aloud, he asked God to meet her spiritual needs. As he prayed, her crying lessened, and when he finished praying, she snuggled closer to him. Pulling his bandanna from his pocket, he dried her tears. Next he quoted from memory several of the sayings of Jesus and the Twenty-Third Psalm, then he reached for the Bible lying on a table by the swing.

"Becoming a Christian isn't difficult because all we have to do is accept Jesus into our heart and lives," he told her. "It's living the way the Bible teaches after our conversion that we find difficult. It seems to me that Paul the apostle summed it up pretty well in the tenth chapter of the book of Romans. 'But what saith it? The word is nigh thee, even in thy mouth, and in thy heart: that is, the word of faith, which we preach; that if thou shalt confess with thy mouth the Lord Jesus, and shalt believe in thine heart that God hath raised him from the dead, thou shalt be saved. For with the heart man believeth unto righteousness; and with the mouth confession is made unto salvation.' "

"What's the reason for using *thou* and *thee*?" she said. "I feel as if I'm reading Shakespeare."

Allen wasn't sure he was capable of answering, but if he took her to Reverend Spencer, this time of opportunity might be lost. Praying for guidance, he said, "I'm not much of a scholar of any kind. However, it's my understanding that the Bible most of us use today was translated from Hebrew and Greek manuscripts during the reign of King James of England in the seventeenth century."

Turning in his Bible to the book of John, Allen read another scripture. " 'Verily, verily, I say unto you, he that heareth my word, and believeth on him that sent me, hath everlasting life, and shall not come into condemnation; but is passed from death unto life.' "

Dora sniffed. "I think I understand, but it seems so simple. Anyone could do that."

Choosing his words carefully, Allen said, "It *is* simple to choose to follow Jesus. The difficult part is the daily living, when our faith has to impact the way we live. For someone who's searching for faith in God, I always suggest that the book of John is the best book to read." He handed her the Bible. "Take this. I have another Bible. If you read something you don't understand, ask Maude or me. I also think you should seek counseling from Reverend Spencer. I'll admit there are many sayings in the Bible I don't understand, and I've been a follower for several years. So don't get discouraged. Unless you're reading Psalms, I'd suggest that you not read in the Old Testament at first."

She leaned over and kissed his cheek. "I don't know what I ever did before you came into my life," she said. "And now I have another project I want you to help with."

Allen rolled his eyes in Maude's direction and feigned a groan. "Now what?"

"It's Kitty. I can't get the child off my mind."

"She's not much of a child now. She's only seventeen, true, but she's old for her years. She and Timothy are good friends—perhaps too good for her age. She comes to see him sometimes."

"I wish we could do something about her injury. There's a doctor in New York, a friend of our family, who specializes in that kind of affliction. I've written to him about her case, and he's volunteered to perform the surgery without any charge, but she'd have to go to New York. I'll pay for her passage and her mother's to New York, and they can stay in that apartment you slept in while Kitty recuperates."

Allen smiled fondly. "Got it all worked out, have you?"

"Not all of it. As usual, I can't do it without your help. She doesn't know me very well, but would you go to New York with her?"

Allen shook his head. "With Ted Morgan still hanging around, it isn't a good time for both of us to leave the textile mill. Her mother should go with her, but who's going to take care of her brothers and sisters when their mother is away?"

"That's not a problem," Maude said. "Many of the neighbors would watch out for the other children, if necessary, but Kitty's grandmother lives in Asheville. I think she'd come and stay with them or take them to her home. If not, I'll stay with the children."

"So you think it's a good idea?" Dora asked Allen.

"Of course."

"I wish you would go to New York with us. Situations might turn up that I couldn't deal with."

He shook his head. "Both of us shouldn't be away at the same time. I still don't trust Morgan. He's moved to Asheville, but I've seen him here in town a few times, too."

"Do you actually think he would try to damage the mill?"

"I don't know, but I distrust him to the extent that I won't leave town right now. Her mother should be with her, but if you can convince Mrs. Franklin to permit the operation and go to New York, we'll work out the other details."

"Why does any situation sound easy when you're involved?" Dora stated, and Allen shifted his gaze from her luminous dark eyes.

"I'm a sucker," he countered. "You usually manage to talk me into schemes I'd never tackle on my own."

When Kitty's youngest sister contracted the chicken pox the day before they were to go to New York for the operation, Mrs. Franklin said she needed to stay at home and take care of the child. Truth be told, Dora figured the woman probably didn't want to go, but neither did Dora want to assume full responsibility for the child's surgery. She had a lawyer prepare an affidavit to approve the surgery, which Mrs. Franklin signed. Using her new-found faith, she prayed that circumstances would permit Allen to accompany her. When Dora asked him again to go with her, he finally agreed, trusting a very dependable foreman to manage the mill during the two weeks they would be gone. Allen wouldn't have gone under any circumstances if Ted Morgan was still hanging around Asheville, but when he learned that the man had been arrested for a bank robbery and sent to prison for two years, Allen felt free to leave for a short time. Maude also accompanied them, intending to spend some time with her relatives while they were in New York.

The excitement of riding on a train for the first time kept Kitty entranced as they traveled from Asheville to Charleston. She was such a sweet girl as well as being pretty with a neat little figure. Dora was happy to help the girl to a better way of life. Her coppery hair hung over her shoulders, and her dark brown eyes sparkled as she looked at the broad fields and elegant houses they saw along the way. Since they had to make an overnight stop in Washington, DC, Dora suggested they spend a few hours touring the capital city before they boarded a train to New York.

Allen arranged for them to take a tour of Washington on a motorized streetcar, which was a treat for him as well as for Kitty. To her, the city seemed like a dream place, but he and Dora compared it to New York City, which was much more advanced than the capital city. On their tour they learned the town had grown quickly in the 1880s, but it still had dirt roads and lacked basic sanitation. The area was swampy and unhealthy to such an extent that some members of Congress suggested moving the capital farther west, but President Grant refused to consider such a proposal.

Although up to that point, Kitty hadn't seemed to be frightened of the ordeal she faced, when they arrived in New York and took a carriage to the six-story stone hospital, she seemed terrified. When they entered the spacious waiting room, she leaned against Allen and tears filled her eyes.

"Oh my," she whispered. "I'm scared. I want my mother. I've been crippled all my life, and I'm used to it now. Let's go home."

Dora looked hopelessly at Allen. He took Kitty's hand and led her to a nearby room that had several benches. He sat down and put his arm around Kitty's shoulders.

"There's nothing to be afraid of," he said soothingly. "You've been a brave girl so far. Your mother would be so disappointed if you go home without having the surgery. Besides, you won't have an operation today. You're just here for an examination and to find out when the surgery will be. Let's talk to the Lord about it."

Dora took Kitty's hand and held it while Allen prayed. "God, bring peace to Kitty's heart. Open her mind so she will realize how much better her life will be when she's free from pain and will be walking like the rest of us do. Calm her spirit, and help her to trust You for healing and the victory from fear. Amen."

The prayer seemed to calm Kitty, and they stayed with her, each of them holding one of her hands, until she was ready to be taken to the examination room. Dora was allowed to accompany her, and when they returned an hour later, Allen thought that Kitty seemed more relaxed. The surgeon had already set aside a time for the operation, which would be the next day.

Allen slept in the apartment downstairs, and although Dora wasn't accustomed to sleeping with anyone, she arranged for Kitty to sleep with her. Tired from the long trip from Fairfield, however, she slept better than she thought she would. The doctor had given them some medication for Kitty to take before she arrived at the hospital. Somewhat docile after that, she didn't seem nearly as uneasy as she'd been the day before, but she did cry most of the time while they waited.

About an hour passed before the nurse came for Kitty. She looked frightened and was reluctant to leave them.

"Ain't you going with me?" she cried, at first refusing to leave her chair, still holding Allen's hand. No doubt the nurse had experience with reluctant patients, for she quietly persuaded Kitty that she must go.

Dora leaned over and kissed her forehead before the nurse took her hand and led her from the waiting room. Then Allen had another crying female to console when Dora's eyes filled with tears. He put his arm around her waist as they sat down to wait. She leaned her head on his shoulder and whispered, "I don't know how I ever lived before you came into my life."

Allen had his own thoughts along that subject, but he knew his relationship with Dora could never be more than friendship, so he didn't comment. Instead he said, "We'll probably have a long wait, so why don't you take a nap? We didn't get much sleep on the train. And we're going to have a week of this because one of us will need to be with her all the time. A place like this is bound to intimidate a girl like Kitty, who's never been away from home before."

Sniffing, Dora said, "She must miss her mother terribly."

Thinking that Dora would make a wonderful mother, he said, "You're doing all right. Mrs. Franklin would have been miserable in a big hospital like this. It's a pity she couldn't be with her daughter, but I think she prefers it this way."

He leaned his head on hers, never expecting to go to sleep himself, but it must have been an hour later when he wakened. His arm was numb, and he wakened Dora when he took his arm from her waist to get the circulation started again. A hostess came by with a tray offering them coffee and cookies, which revived them somewhat, and they settled down for a long wait.

At the end of several hours when the surgeon came to the waiting room, Dora squeezed his hand, and it was obvious that she was concerned over the outcome. She'd persuaded Kitty and her mother that surgery would give the girl a new lease on life, and she would feel responsible if the operation wasn't successful.

Shaking hands with them, the surgeon said, "The patient came through the surgery well, and she'll be in a room in a couple of hours. She should be ready to leave the hospital in a week, but she'll have to use a crutch until her leg heals. We need to teach her how to walk to prevent falling. It will be several weeks before you can take her home to North Carolina."

Allen smothered a groan, thinking he couldn't stay in New York that long. With both Dora and him away, all kinds of problems could occur at the textile mill. Timothy would do everything he could, as would the foreman, but Allen couldn't rid himself of the notion that they hadn't seen the last of Ted Morgan.

Chapter 10

Although Dora obviously didn't want him to leave, she must have realized he was needed more in North Carolina than with her. He stayed for a week until Kitty was released from the hospital, then he took a southbound train. As soon as the surgery was over, Dora had sent a special delivery letter to Mrs. Franklin, but Allen knew that Kitty's mother would be uneasy until the girl was home. Although he was eager to check on events at the mill, when he got off the train in Fairfield, he went directly to the Franklin home. Mrs. Franklin had already received Dora's letter, but Allen updated her on the girl's recovery before he went to the mill office.

When he walked in, Timothy was laboring over one of the ledgers. When he saw Allen, a comical expression of relief spread over the boy's face, and he wrapped Allen in a big bear hug. "I've never been so happy to see anybody in my life," he said.

Allen disentangled himself from Timothy's clutch. "What's wrong? Have you had any trouble?"

"Nary a bit of trouble. According to the foreman everything is moving smoothly, but I've worried all the time what I'd do if we did have some trouble. I tell you this kind of life isn't for me. I'm still planning to go west to seek my fortune. I haven't had a decent night's sleep since you left."

"Then that makes two of us."

"And Kitty is still doing all right?"

"Yes, I didn't leave until she'd learned to walk on the crutches. She'll have to use them for a while. It will probably be a month before they can come home."

Timothy groaned. "Four whole weeks! But at least you're home, so I can go back to the farm."

If Allen still harbored doubts of how much he loved Dora, not seeing her for a month removed all doubts. He haunted the train station when a train was due, hoping she and Kitty would be on it. As soon as he'd arrived home, he'd sent a letter to Dora, and he hoped she would answer soon. Every day he went to the post office hoping for a message from her. When he did receive a letter saying that they would return to Fairfield within a week, he felt better. However, he realized that he was never going to be satisfied if Dora wasn't where he could see her every day.

Should he ask her to marry him? Sometimes the expression on her face and the warmth radiating from her eyes led him to believe that she loved him. A few times he'd been tempted to talk to her about marriage, but each time he thought about it, he cringed. When he considered proposing to her, the word *millionaire* popped into his mind, and he figured most people would think he was marrying her for her money. Certainly her father would. The days passed endlessly, and he remembered how Dora had embraced him when he showed up at her New York apartment. He knew how she felt now. He prayed he wouldn't do anything foolish when he met the train on her return.

Finally, he received a message that they were scheduled to arrive on the evening train within three days. He spread the word, and a crowd gathered to welcome Kitty home. When the train rolled into the station, a conductor stepped off first. Kitty appeared in the doorway, using a cane for support rather than the crutch she'd been using the last time he had seen her, and the conductor helped her down the steps.

With her free hand she waved and threw kisses at her friends and neighbors. Mrs. Franklin stepped forward, with her five other children beside her, and waited for Kitty. A lightweight brace was still on her leg, but she maneuvered the three train steps easily. Allen noted tears in her eyes, but he turned as his beloved came down the steps. She looked over the crowd until she saw him, and a ready smile spread across her beautiful face. He took her hand and helped her down the last step.

"Welcome home," he whispered. "I've missed you."

"Same here," she said. Looking around the large crowd and to the town beyond, she continued, "Oh, it's good to be home."

Hearing her say those words brought happiness to his heart.

"When you sent word that Maude was going to stay in New York until after Christmas, I hired a reliable woman in Asheville to help you." He picked up her bags. "I'll take these to your house. I told her that you'd be here today, and I'm sure she'll have everything cozy for you. She's preparing supper."

"Will you eat with me?" Dora asked. "I don't like to eat alone."

Allen grinned sheepishly. "I told her to prepare enough for two."

"Is everything all right at the mill?"

"Yes. I think you'll be pleased when you check the finances. You didn't make a lot of money, but your income was more than expenses. I am worried about one situation, however. Ted Morgan has escaped from prison. He killed a guard in doing so, and the police are diligently searching for him, but so far he's still on the loose."

"You're afraid for me, right?"

"Of course! That's why I'm sorry Maude didn't come home with you, so you wouldn't be living alone. I'm going to be uneasy until he's caught."

"Don't you think you're in danger, too?"

"Sure, but he'd only shoot me. I doubt that's what he would do to you."

It was only a month until Christmas when Dora first approached Allen about what she should do for the mill workers for the holiday season. "Should I give them a bonus? Do they have a holiday then? What should I do?"

"I don't know," Allen said, flipping the calendar to December. "I'm sure there's always an extra holiday of some sort, but I'll find out. Christmas comes on a weekday, so I'd suggest you give them an extra day or two."

"I've been thinking that I could make their Christmas Day a whole week from Christmas through New Year's Day, with pay. That could be their Christmas bonus. Do you think that's generous enough?"

"More than generous! But if you do that this year, you'd be setting a precedent that they'd expect every year. I don't mean to pry into your affairs, but can you afford to be so generous?"

"The auditors tell me that we've made more profit this year than the mill had cleared the past two years. I think we can afford it. I'm willing to try it, but I won't if you think it isn't a good idea."

"Are you going to New York for Christmas?" he asked.

She shook her head. "No, but I've insisted that Mattie go and spend time with her family. As long as my grandmother lived, I spent Christmas week with her, but now that she's gone, I've usually spent the day at home. Mrs. Vanderbilt has invited me to spend the day with them, but some of their relatives are coming so I told her I had other plans, which means I'll probably spend the day at home."

Although Allen usually spent Christmas Day with his cousins Vance and Evelyn Bolden in Canaan, he had no intention of leaving her alone. He persuaded her to go with him to spend the holiday with the Boldens. He was also worried about leaving the mill. If there was any trouble, he didn't want Dora to be in Fairfield alone. He hired several reliable men to watch the place, and with Timothy also on guard he didn't think he had too much to worry about. He would have taken Timothy with them, but he wanted to stay with Kitty and her family. So they set out for Canaan without concern for the property.

The weather was mild for December, but Allen had put curtains on his buggy to protect Dora from the cold weather. Fortunately the wind was blowing from the south today, and it was cozy in the buggy. Glancing sideways at Dora, Allen smiled, wondering how he was so fortunate to have this woman favor him. She wore a full-length fur coat and a tam and muff to match. The outfit must have cost a fortune, at least more money than he'd make in a year's time.

Dora had been looking forward to this trip, and she was obviously enjoying the evergreens that were decorated with tufts of snow that had fallen throughout the night. It was a winter wonderland, and if Allen had needed anything else to put him in the Christmas spirit, Dora sitting beside him, looking as if she'd just stepped out of a New York department store dressed in all her finery, would have done it. Her eyes roved the countryside, obviously enjoying the winter day to its fullest.

"Now, why are you looking at me like that?" she demanded. Her even teeth flashed in a gentle smile.

"Oh, I don't know—maybe wondering why I'm such a lucky guy—to be celebrating Christmas with you. We've known each other more than a year now, and you're so much a part of my life I don't know what I'll do when you aren't around anymore."

She lifted her chin in a haughty gesture that reminded him of her father. "What makes you think I'm going anywhere?"

"It just stands to reason that you won't be content to spend the rest of your life here. When I compare your lifestyle in New York with Fairfield, I can't imagine how you could possibly be happy in a rural area like ours."

"Well, I'm not going to leave North Carolina this week, so let's forget that. It was gracious of your relatives to invite me."

"I wasn't about to leave you in Fairfield on Christmas Day, especially when I know that Vance and Evelyn will be happy that you're with me."

"Share something about them so I'll know what to expect."

"Vance Bolden is my cousin, although his father was much more prosperous than mine. His family owned a plantation in South Carolina since the mid-1700s, but my father was a sharecropper in the neighborhood. After the War Between the States, Southerners, especially those who'd fought for the Confederacy, had nothing left. When Union soldiers invaded the South, they destroyed a lot of property to punish Southerners for seceding from the Union. Vance was married before the war, but while he was serving in the Confederacy, his wife and son died."

"So Evelyn is a second wife?"

Nodding his head, he explained, "And in my opinion, a much better wife for Vance than his first one. After the war ended, he tried to rebuild the plantation, but many Yankees moved into the state and bought property the Southerners couldn't afford to keep. The Boldens had never owned slaves, of course, and they'd been treated more like sharecroppers—receiving a portion of what they raised on their acreage. Vance's maternal relatives owned property in this area, and his father dreamed of leaving the past behind them and starting anew in a new region. When his father died, Vance sold the property and moved here. Many of his neighbors came, too, and they established the settlement of Canaan several years ago. Most of the immigrants have prospered there, either buying homes in town or settling on farms."

"And you came with them?"

"Yes, my father was a sharecropper, too—that means he didn't own any land, but worked for the plantation owners. I was the oldest kid in the family, and I knew there wasn't any future for me in that area. I wanted to make a new start, and I paid my way westward by helping Vance and Evelyn with their wagons and horses. I lived in Canaan a few years then came to the Asheville area."

"You seem to have the wanderlust. Have you considered leaving here?"

"At first I intended to go west, possibly as far as California to seek my fortune in the gold fields. After I bought the farm and found I could earn a living with my carpentry work, I haven't thought of leaving. Wanderlust must be a Bolden family characteristic. As you know, Timothy has mentioned that he will probably move westward."

"Will you try to stop him?"

Allen glanced at her in surprise. "Why should I? I'm not his guardian."

The miles passed quickly. Sometimes they'd ride a long distance without comment, although Dora had many questions about what kind of trees they saw along the roadside and about the history of the area. They stopped a couple of times to stretch their legs and to view the mountains to the west.

When they were closer to Canaan, Allen said, "Probably I should tell you about Evelyn, Vance's wife, too. She has an interesting past. She and her husband worked at a mission in London, and the Lord called them to be missionaries among the Cherokee Indians, whose homeland is in this area. The ship they traveled on wrecked off the South Carolina coast. Vance just happened to be on a nearby island when that happened, and although her husband was drowned, Vance was able to save Evelyn's life. She was with child, and because of the storm Vance couldn't go to his plantation for help. With Vance's assistance she gave birth to twins on the island while the storm raged around them."

She nodded. "Goodness. How terrible, but how wonderful, too. It seems like a fairy tale."

"Well, to make a long story short, Vance and Evelyn married, and they've lived 'happily afterward.' And I do mean they're happy. They were meant for each other, but it took a hurricane to bring them together. In addition to the twins, they have a child of their own."

"Do you believe that?"

Allen glanced at her. "Believe what?"

"That when they're born certain people are meant for each other?"

"I'm not sure. In some cases, I do—like Vance and Evelyn. But that's just my opinion—I don't have any biblical passage to back up what I believe."

"What about us?"

Laughing, Allen said, "Don't start that again! We're friends, but no more than that. We're too different to ever get along. Sometimes when I see poorly matched husbands and wives who seem to share a good marriage, I believe that God has a sense of humor." They were heading toward a subject he didn't want to discuss, so Allen was glad that they arrived in Canaan, which took Dora's attention for the time being. He suspected, however, that he hadn't heard the last of the subject. It must be the mystery of the ages—why a woman like her would favor him.

"What a quaint little town!" Dora said. "And it's only been here twenty years?"

He nodded, but devoted all of his attention to his skittish horses. Several other horses were tied along Main Street, and he had to watch his team closely to prevent a ruckus if any of the other animals were as cantankerous. Canaan didn't cover much territory, so they were soon out of town, and in a short time Allen pointed ahead to a two-story redbrick house.

"That's where we're going."

"Why, it's a mansion!" Dora exclaimed. "Wouldn't it be wonderful to have a home like that?"

Recalling the picture he'd seen of the Porter mansion near New York City, he was somewhat surprised that Dora would consider this so noteworthy. Allen didn't comment, but he was pleased that she liked the area. Hopefully she would also enjoy this Christmas visit with his closest friends.

"That's a lovely home," Dora said, and her eyes were alight with interest.

"You're referring to the building, of course, and I agree that it's quite a mansion. But it's what goes on inside the house that makes it so special. Evelyn and Vance love one another so much that it's always a blessing for me to visit them. Since I was separated from my parents after I came north, I've been blessed because Evelyn has never failed to include me in their family observances and holidays."

"I'm still not sure I should have come," Dora said, and her forehead wrinkled into a slight frown. "Christmas is family time, so I hope they won't mind my presence."

"They won't. You have no worries. You met their daughter, Marie, at the Vanderbilt's open house."

"I sort of remember her, but there were so many

strangers there, I didn't get to know anyone very well." She smiled. "Except you, of course!"

Favoring her with an oblique glance, he asked, "Are you sorry?"

With a mysterious smile, she answered, "What do you think?" Then in a more serious tone, Dora added, "No, I'm not sorry. Coming to North Carolina has changed my life. In fact, I don't feel that I'd ever really 'lived' before. I spent years wrapped up in myself, never thinking much about the future or anyone else. You've talked to me about having a new birth spiritually, but I also believe that I had a new birth psychologically."

When Allen pulled his team to a halt in front of the brick house, a black man came from a nearby house to take charge of the team.

"Hello, Jasper," Allen said as he stepped from the buggy. "Do you have time to look after the team?"

"Yes sir, I sure do."

Allen lifted his hand to help Dora step from the buggy. "I brought my friend, Dora Porter, with me. Jasper and his wife, Fannie, have worked for the Boldens most of their lives."

Jasper tipped his hat. "Pleased to meet you, ma'am." Jasper set out their two suitcases before he climbed into the buggy and headed the team toward the barn, located on a knoll behind the house.

When Allen opened the gate in the picket fence, the front door opened and a tall, handsome man stepped out. Two women followed him from the house.

"I see you brought company, Allen," the man called. "Come in out of the cold, and introduce me to this lovely lady."

"This is my friend, Dora Porter. She owns the textile mill in Fairfield."

Allen's heart swelled with pride in Dora while Vance and Evelyn welcomed her so warmly. She didn't seem ill at ease, nor was she condescending, and goodness knows she had reason to be if she wanted to. This was a spacious and elegant house, but nothing compared to what her father owned.

Motioning to the woman beside him, Allen said, "This is Marie."

Dora greeted Marie, saying that she remembered her. "Allen said you wouldn't mind if I joined you today," she said to Evelyn. "I'd have been alone in Fairfield if I hadn't come here."

"You are surely welcome," Evelyn said. "Allen has written about your work in Fairfield, and it will be good for you to have a few days away from the mill."

Allen and Dora were served coffee and pastries immediately, and afterward Evelyn asked Marie to prepare an upstairs bedroom for their guest.

After Marie and Dora went upstairs to the bedroom, Allen addressed Evelyn. "Thank you for allowing Dora to come today."

Evelyn smiled. "Should we expect an announcement from the two of you before long?"

Allen lifted his hand. "Whoa! Don't get any ideas like that."

"Why not?" Evelyn asked. "It's obvious you love one another."

"That's true, but as far as I'm concerned, it will never go any further than that." His two friends looked skeptical. "Evelyn's father is one of the richest men in New York, and although he's mad at Dora now and has threatened to disinherit her, I doubt he will do it because she's his only child. Even if he does, Dora's maternal grandmother left her a fortune, and she used that money to renovate the mill, which is probably worth close to a million dollars. I can't even guess the extent of her finances, and I don't want to know. She depends on me to steer her in the right direction in dealing with her employees, and I'm glad to do it, but I'll never ask her to marry me."

When Evelyn started to speak again, Vance shook his head. "I can understand your situation. I'd probably feel the same way if I were in your position."

"That isn't logical," Evelyn argued. "When you married me, I had no worldly possessions at all, and I had two children, which you took as your own. Why is it any different for a woman to have money and still marry someone who doesn't have any?"

Vance smiled sheepishly. "I don't know, but that's the way it is."

"Because it makes men feel inferior," Evelyn retorted, and her dark eyes flashed angrily. "Allen, you might not bring a million dollars into the marriage, but you own property and you have an occupation that keeps you busy. You don't have to use her money, but I beg you, Allen, don't let selfish pride ruin both of your lives."

Considering it time to change the subject, Allen said, "You've heard that my brother Timothy has come to live with me."

"Yes, I saw the boy when he was working for our neighbor," Vance said. "I gathered he intended on heading to California."

Smiling, Allen responded, "That was the original idea. He met a girl in Fairfield who may have changed his mind."

Allen had attended several Christmas celebrations in Canaan, and tonight was extra-special because he would have the opportunity to share the season with Dora. Since she'd so recently turned her heart and life over to the Lord, this would be her first Christmas to actually appreciate the true meaning of the season. They drove into Canaan in his buggy for the Christmas church service, and she moved close to him.

"Are you cold?" he asked, wondering how she

could possibly be cold in the floor-length, elegant fur coat she wore.

"Not really," she said teasingly, "but I thought this would be a good time to snuggle close to you. I didn't want to miss the opportunity."

Although Allen liked having her so close, he didn't say so. Instead he asked, "Do you like my friends?"

She nodded her head against his shoulder. "Very much. I especially like them because they've been so kind to you."

"I didn't have much kindness when I was growing up. When my parents produced a new baby about every year and I was the oldest of the brood, my mother understandingly couldn't spend much time with me."

"Did you resent that?"

"At the time, yes I did. I've gotten over it."

They had seen the town's evergreen decorations when they'd entered Canaan in the afternoon, but now with candles burning in every window and in sheltered nooks along the streets, the area looked like a fairyland. The fact that a lazy snowfall was drifting slowly toward the earth added to the magic of the evening.

A few blocks from the center of town, Allen guided his team into a wide area where a log church nestled in a grove of towering evergreen trees. He tied the horses to one of the trees and came to lift

Dora down from the buggy. The door to the church was open, and several people were converging on the building. Many of them were former acquaintances of Allen's, and he heartily returned their "Merry Christmas" greetings.

A woman sat at an organ playing music that was unfamiliar to Dora. Allen hummed the tune and sang a few lines as they moved inside the building and found room for them to sit on a pew halfway up the aisle. As they'd entered the candlelit sanctuary, Dora sensed a peace in her heart and mind she'd never experienced before. Why hadn't somebody told her before about the meaning of Christmas? Why had her father ignored the Christian faith all his life? She knew that he and her mother had been married in a church, so what had caused him to forsake the faith? Dora was still so new to the gift of prayer she'd received a few weeks earlier that she hardly knew how to pray. Did she have to bow her head to pray like several of the others in the building were doing? She reached over and touched Allen's hand, and he wrapped his warm fingers around hers. When he bowed his head, so did she.

She'd heard Allen pray several times and, the few times she'd gone to church, she'd listened intently to the preacher's words. "God, I want to do and say the right thing," she prayed, "partly because I know it's what I should do, but also because Allen so desperately wants me to grow spiritually. Will it take a lifetime?"

Although she spoke so quietly that he couldn't have heard what she was saying, Allen lifted her hand and kissed it. Wouldn't it be wonderful if they could serve the Lord as man and wife? He obviously loved her, so it was only his pride about her wealth that kept them apart. She was half-tempted to notify her father that she was renouncing ownership of the textile mill and returning it to him. That way she would be penniless. Allen could sell his farm for enough money to finance a trip to California, where they could live on the money he had. Now that she owned the textile mill, she wondered if she'd ever travel to faraway places again. Having seen all of Europe that she wanted to see, Dora had planned that her next big trip would be California.

Before she had more time to think about such a far-fetched idea, the pastor started his sermon. "In order to observe the birth of the Christ Child as we should, it's important that we look into the Old Testament as well as the New Testament. For years prophets and kings had foretold the coming of the Messiah without any sign of the promised one. Years passed, and most of the faithful ones who had looked for the Messiah had almost lost hope.

"When the time did come, God chose a young girl through whom His magnificent plan would be revealed. Isaiah's prophecy in the ninth chapter of the book by his name was very plain as to the purpose. 'For unto us a child is born, unto us a son is given: and the government shall be upon his shoulder: and his name shall be called Wonderful, Counsellor, the mighty God, the everlasting Father, the Prince of Peace. Of the increase of his government and peace there shall be no end, upon the throne of David, and upon his kingdom, to order it, and to establish it with judgment and with justice from henceforth even for ever. The zeal of the Lord of hosts will perform this.' "

Trying to figure out what this really meant, Dora missed some of the pastor's sermon, but focused again when he said, "In obedience, Joseph and Mary traveled to Bethlehem and found no lodging except in a stable where Jesus Christ was born. The news of this birth spread quickly when angels announced the birth of Jesus to shepherds, who went immediately to Bethlehem and found Jesus, the Son of God, lying in a manger. The shepherds spread this wonderful news to everyone they met—telling what had happened and the message the angels revealed to them. All who heard it were amazed to learn that God had come to earth in the body of a baby.

"Several months later, others came to worship the Christ Child. In their studies of the stars and universe, wise men from eastern lands had seen the unusual star and knew it could mean only one thing—a king had been born! Although they didn't know it, this was a king whose reign would be forever.

"The Hebrew people had waited for centuries for the promised one, never expecting that He would arrive in such a humble way. They expected a king robed in royal splendor. Jesus came as a servant. He was born in a stable. They had also believed that the whole world would exalt the Christ Child, yet he was rejected by many because his birth didn't meet their expectations."

The enlightening sermon continued. Occasionally someone would cough or a baby whimpered, but otherwise the congregation's attention was focused on the message. Although it was a new message to her, Dora figured that most of the people had often heard the story, but apparently the "old" message became a "new" message each Christmas Eve.

"There was something miraculous about the angels' visit to the shepherds that night," the pastor continued. "The glory of the Lord shone around them, and it was a night the shepherds weren't likely to forget."

The audience stood for the closing hymn, which started, "It came upon a midnight clear, that glorious song of old, from angels bending near the earth to touch their harps of gold."

No one was using a hymnal, but the minister led the congregation from the pulpit as they sang several verses of the song. Dora hummed the melody, and her inner self was warmed by the message and the fellowship of these dedicated people. After the benediction, no one seemed in any hurry to go home. Allen held Dora's hand and led her through the crowd, introducing her to numerous people, whose names she didn't even try to remember. It had been a long day, and she was thankful when Allen finally left the building and they headed toward Sunrise Manor.

Christmas had always been a commercial event for Dora, and she was more in the Christmas spirit this year than she'd ever been. She'd spent enormous amounts of money to buy gifts for the servants, her father, and friends. She had given a bonus to the workers, and she'd bought a watch for Allen, hoping that he'd never realize how much she paid for it. When he told her who would be at the Boldens' for Christmas, she had gone into Asheville and purchased gifts for the family.

They returned to the Bolden home before the family did, and she gave Allen the watch while they were alone. He was obviously pleased.

"I have a gift for you, too," he said. "But it's at the farm, and you'll have to wait a few days before you can claim it."

"Are you going to tell me what it is?"

"Sure, if you want to know. I'm giving you one of my horses. I have six or seven good riding horses—

you can take your pick of any of them. Any time you want to ride when I'm not available, you can go to the farm. Timothy is usually there, so he can help you with the saddle. You may want to take your rides close to the farm buildings for the time being."

"Oh, thank you. I've never owned a horse, although I took riding lessons at stables outside the city." She touched his hand, hoping that he would respond. When he turned away, she asked, "Why do you want me to stay close to the farmstead?"

"I don't think we've heard the last of Ted Morgan. He hates both of us—probably me more than he does you. He's the kind who would mistreat you to get even with me. I don't like for you to be alone at all, as long as he's still hanging around."

"So that's the reason you brought me to visit the Boldens!"

"Partly," he said, adding sheepishly, "but I didn't want to go half a week without seeing you either."

Chapter 11

On the return trip to Fairfield, Dora seemed quieter than usual. Allen, preoccupied with thoughts of the coming year and projects they had contracted for at the mill, wasn't talkative either. After they'd traveled a long distance, Dora said, "I have an idea."

Allen feigned a groan and covered his eyes with his left hand. "If I had a dollar for every time I've heard you say that in the past year, I'd be a millionaire, too."

Obviously annoyed, Dora said, "Allen! I've been thinking about this for two or three months, and I want your opinion."

"All right. No more joking. I haven't disappointed you yet, have I?"

"Only in one very important situation."

Knowing very well what she meant, he answered, "All right. If it isn't anything of a personal nature, but has the interest of the mill at stake, I'll not disappoint you this time either."

"Do you know how many of our mill employees can't even write their names? When they sign a receipt for their salaries, all they can do is make an *X*. It's incredible."

"Incredible, I'll grant you, but not unusual. Very few adults in this state have had an opportunity to get much schooling, but I don't know what you can do about it. I think it will take a statewide election to bring education to everyone."

"Where did you learn to read and write?" she asked.

"On the Bolden plantation where my father worked. Vance's father provided education for his workers, black and white alike."

"I know a retired teacher, Lester Holdredge, in New York, who would probably welcome the opportunity to spend some time here in the mountains. You met him on your first visit to my home."

With a grimace, Allen answered, "I remember him very well. I thought you were probably engaged to him, and I felt as if I'd been kicked in the stomach by a mule when I walked into your apartment and saw him. I'd been looking forward to seeing you so much, I thought the train would never get to New York, and when I got to your apartment, you were with another man."

She made a face at him. "Oh really! He's old enough to be my father. I've known him since I was a child. In fact, his wife used to take me home with them. One of my earliest memories was when Lester used to dangle me on his knee. He's much older than I am, and we don't have much in common. He's my father's friend, not mine."

"Maybe so, but it still upset me. Even though you'd hugged me, I was still angry. Back then I didn't trust you very much. I know better now."

"Let's forget that. My point is, Lester is a retired schoolteacher and a widower without any children. He was educated in New York's finest colleges, and he could have had most any position he wanted. Instead, he chose to teach in elementary schools. His wife was a teacher, too, and they went into slum districts and taught children who would never have had an education otherwise. After his wife died a few years ago, he's been very lonely. I'm sure he would gladly come here to teach these men, and he'd pay his own expenses. What do you think?"

"Sounds like a great idea to me. Many of the women haven't had any schooling either."

"Who would I contact to get permission?"

"I'm not sure, but since these are adults, I don't

know that it would be necessary to get permission from the board of education. Why don't you talk to Reverend Spencer about it and go from there? Since you're willing to give the men time off from work to go to school, it wouldn't be a matter you would have to take up with the mayor. However, it might be wise to have the town sponsor the school—and you could provide any necessary money."

"Is there a vacant building we could use?"

"Several of them."

Dora seemed to be seriously considering the situation. "Should I discuss this with the mayor or other town officials before I do anything else?"

"I don't know that would be necessary. If you think your friend will come without charge, it isn't a project that will cost the town any money, unless you want the city government to pay for the books."

"No, there wouldn't be any charge. If Lester agrees to come, I'm sure he will provide the books. So you think it's a good idea?"

"I'm not paid to think," he said with a mischievous grin. "As usual, you make the decisions, and I do what you tell me to do."

Frowning, she cuffed him on the shoulder. "You always make it sound as if I'm ordering you around. I've tried to get you to take the initiative, and you won't do it."

"I'm a better follower than a leader. You have the brains in this business."

"Ha!" she said sarcastically. "You like to make me think I'm the boss, but I notice that I usually end up doing what you want me to."

"I *will* make one suggestion, or maybe two," Allen said. "It might be well for you to talk to the workers about this project before you send for the teacher. Also, you would probably have to give them time off from work to take the classes because most of them have chores at home after they leave the mill. That would cut into the mill's profit."

"I'll give it some thought and come up with a schedule before I talk to them. I can't imagine what it would be like to not be able to read and write."

Although Allen tried his best to hide his love for Dora, sometimes his emotions took over, and he couldn't treat her in the offhand attitude he usually maintained. He stopped the horses, tied the reins to the side of the buggy, and pulled her into a tight embrace.

"You're a pretty special person, do you know that? I'll venture to say that there isn't another woman in this country with the wealth you have who would have the interest in a group of uneducated, poor people like you do. After I've seen how you live in New York and know your background, it amazes me."

Her eyes were full of such love and tenderness that it made his heart ache with loneliness. She clung to him, and knowing that she really did love him, Allen hugged her to him in an emotion too deep for words. He almost proposed to her on the spot, but pride intervened again. He kissed her forehead, released her, and continued the journey to Fairfield.

Once she'd conceived an idea and Allen had approved it, Dora wasn't one to postpone a project. She composed a letter to Lester Holdredge.

Dear Lester:

Help! We have a need in Fairfield that I believe you can fill. The local schools are adequate for the education of children, but I have learned that many of the male employees in our textile mill can neither read nor write. Would you be willing to come to North Carolina and work with these men? Allen says that I should determine how many of the men would be interested in going to school before you come, but even if we can only help educate a few of them, it will be worthwhile. I wanted to learn if you agreed before I mention it locally.

Please don't mention this to Father, but I'll admit that I've invested almost all of my capital in the mill, so we couldn't pay you much. If you are interested, you will need to bring textbooks. And remember, you'll be teaching

*illiterate adults. Even if we help only two or
three men, it will be worth it.*

*Sincerely,
Dora*

Two weeks later, she received a telegram from
Lester.

Bored stiff. Will arrive in two weeks. No salary needed or wanted.

By the time Lester arrived, Allen and Dora had
rented a one-story house where Lester could live
and teach school. One room was large enough for a
classroom, and Allen borrowed several desks from
the local high school to furnish the room. Only
three men agreed to attend the school, but that was
a beginning and enough to encourage Dora. On the
opening day of school, when Dora slipped quietly
into the classroom and heard grown men haltingly
reading, "Baby Ray had a dog. Baby Ray had a cat,"
her reward was complete.

Chapter 12

Ringing bells disturbed Allen's sleep, and he bolted out of bed and rushed to the window that faced Fairfield. An occasional streak of fire burst into the air, and he pinpointed the fire near the textile mill. Timothy rushed out of the other bedroom.

"That fire's pretty close, huh?" he said.

"Too close! With the rain we had last week, we aren't in danger of grass fires, so there must be a building on fire in Fairfield." Allen pulled on his pants and shrugged into his shirt as he talked. "I'm going to see what's up. I suppose I have a suspicious nature, but I've been expecting trouble."

"From Ted Morgan?"

Allen nodded his head. Running into his bedroom, Timothy said, "Wait until I put on some clothes, and I'll go with you. Every hand will be needed if it's a big fire. You don't suppose it's the textile mill, do you?"

"I hope not, but if not, it's close to the mill," Allen said, his main concern for Dora. Buildings could be replaced, but nothing could compensate for losing her.

By the time Timothy was dressed, Allen had saddled two horses. Timothy straddled one, and Allen swung into the other saddle. Side by side they raced the horses toward town. When they reached Fairfield, a bucket brigade was already working to contain the blazing fire in a machine shop connected to the textile mill by a short, covered walkway. Allen and Timothy had brought buckets with them, and they positioned themselves at the end of the line, dipped water from the creek, and passed it to the men in front of them. They worked steadily, and Allen was impressed by the silence among the people. Intent on their work, the men didn't talk. Children and women stood to one side, some with heads bowed obviously praying while others stared in shocked dismay at the flaming building. As he worked, Allen looked intently at the bystanders, but he couldn't see Dora anywhere.

Still carrying the bucket, he ran toward the women. "Do any of you know where Miss Porter is?"

Several of them shook their heads, but one woman said, "She was here soon after the fire was discovered, and she went to look for Kitty. She cleans the buildings before the other workers arrive, and Miss Porter was afraid she might still be inside."

Nodding his thanks, Allen ran toward the flaming building. Kitty was leaning against a giant pine tree, tears streaking her face as she watched the destruction.

"Have you seen Dora?" Allen shouted above the racket of the fire and shouting workers.

"Not since she pulled me out of the building," Kitty said. "She wanted to know who else was inside. I didn't know, so she may have gone to see if anybody else was in the building."

"Oh dear God, help," Allen prayed as he darted toward the flames.

"Come back! Come back!" someone shouted. "The roof is about ready to collapse."

Heedless of the warning, Allen tied his handkerchief over his mouth and nose and darted into the thick smoke. "Dora! Dora!" he shouted over and over. "Where are you?"

"Here! Here!" He heard her beloved voice and headed in that direction.

"Keep calling until I find you!" he shouted. In spite of the flames, he couldn't see anything. His eyes were stinging from the smoke, but he groped in the darkness trying to determine where she was.

"Allen! Allen!" she cried frantically. "A log has fallen on my leg, and I can't move."

"I can't see anything, my love, so keep calling until I find you."

Allen stumbled in the darkness and fell to his knees more than once. The last time he fell, he crawled on hands and knees following her voice. Reaching her at last, he pushed the log aside and scooped Dora up in his arms. Running as fast as he could, he headed toward the front of the building and plunged through the door to safety. It was none too soon either. As he stumbled toward the road, where many citizens of Fairfield stood staring incredulously as the source of their livelihood was destroyed by flames, the roof of the building collapsed. Smoke and flames soared upward as Allen collapsed on the ground and pulled Dora into his arms.

"Are you hurt?" he questioned weakly. "Do you have any burns?"

"I don't think so," Dora said. She leaned back in his arms. "A log or board of some kind fell on my leg, but I'm not in pain so I can't be hurt very much."

"Let's get married right away," he said, tears running down his face.

Allen hadn't cried since he was a boy, and he didn't know if the smoke or his fear of losing Dora had caused the tears, but he cast his pride aside. Still clasping her in his arms as if he would never let go, he continued, "In those few minutes when I thought I'd lost you, I realized that nothing matters except my love for you. I don't care if you're as rich as that Croesus fellow, I want to marry you and the sooner the better."

"All right," she agreed. "We'll get married today before you change your mind. But you don't have to be concerned about my wealth. Most of my inheritance just went up in flames. I invested almost all of my capital in improving the textile mill. That's why Father is so angry with me. Thank God, though, that I am insured heavily, so we'll be able to rebuild. Let's go."

"Go where?"

"To find Reverend Spencer. I want to take advantage of your proposal before you change your mind."

Reverend Spencer was also working in the bucket brigade, and when the last hint of fire was extinguished, Allen and Dora approached him.

"We want to get married," Allen said.

"Now?" the preacher said, and Allen laughed at the amazed expression on his face.

"Right here and now, if you have your Bible with you," Dora said. "I've been trying for months to get Allen to the altar, and I want to take advantage of his weak moment. He wouldn't marry me because he thought I was too rich." She swept her hand toward the destroyed building. "He doesn't have to worry about that now. It will take all the money I have to start over."

Every able-bodied resident of Fairfield was gathered in the area, many of them now reclining on the ground. Dora felt sure that no one else in the whole world had ever had a wedding like theirs, but she also believed that no other group of people would have been more eager to give their blessing to the union between her and Allen.

It certainly wasn't the kind of wedding she'd dreamed of since she was a child. In her dreams, she always walked beside her father down a long church aisle to be married. She'd never been able to see the face of the man who waited for her at the altar, but she knew now that it had always been Allen.

Instead of the garments she'd envisioned in her youth—satin gown, accessories, and a veil that swept the floor behind her as she approached the altar—today her clothes were stained with smoke and grime, as were the pastor's and all the residents of Fairfield. She knew that her face was as dirty as Allen's and the others. Her hair, which had been neat and tidy when she'd come to work this morning, straggled around her face. Many of the men lay on the grass exhausted from the extreme heat they'd battled to confine the fire to prevent it from spreading to the rest of the town. It seemed such a suspicious fire, as if the flames had started in more than one area of the mill.

Reverend Spencer asked her and Allen to join hands, and he took a small Bible from his pocket.

Dora hadn't considered that they would need witnesses until Timothy and Kitty came to stand beside them. A hush settled over the whole area as the pastor began the ritual.

"Dearly beloved, we are gathered together here in the sight of God and in the presence of these witnesses to join this man and this woman in holy matrimony. This honorable estate, instituted of God, was adorned and beautified by the presence of our Lord Jesus Christ at the marriage in Cana of Galilee."

The pastor continued the brief service, and soon it was time to take their vows. After he asked them to join hands, tears came to Dora's eyes, and she wasn't surprised to see that Allen was tearful also. This was more emotion than she'd ever known him to exhibit, and she lifted his hand and kissed it. Reverend Spencer's next words seemed to sear themselves into Dora's heart, and she knew she would never forget them or this moment.

"I charge you both, as you stand in the presence of God, to remember that only love and loyalty will avail as the foundation of a happy and enduring home. If the solemn vows that you are about to make be kept inviolate, and if steadfastly you seek to do the will of your heavenly Father, your life will be full of peace and joy, and the home that you are establishing will remain through every crisis."

As the pastor asked, "Who gives this woman and man in marriage?" it suddenly dawned on Dora that they didn't have anyone to give them away. Nor did they have a ring. She and Allen exchanged puzzled glances, but the problem was solved when the citizens of Fairfield shouted in unison, "We do!" Their words were followed by a tremendous outpouring of praise as the spectators heartily applauded this unusual ceremony. Momentarily, Dora realized that not only were these folks her employees, but they were also her friends. She couldn't have found this many people in New York who even knew her, let alone be considered as friends.

"Then I pronounce you man and wife," the preacher said. "What God has joined together let no man put asunder. Allen, you may kiss your bride."

He didn't have to be prompted a second time, and in spite of the smoky taste on his lips, Dora had never sensed such a warmth of heart and peace of mind. She had at last found her home in Allen.

After they'd welcomed and received the congratulations of their friends and neighbors, with a stupefied expression on his face, Allen said, "We might have been too hasty. Where are we going to live? And what about a honeymoon?"

Determined to be an obedient wife, rather than to make this decision, Dora said, "I don't have any preference—your house or mine."

"Then why don't I move in with you for the time being? My farmhouse is rather primitive, and I wouldn't expect you to live there. Timothy can continue to live on the farm and take care of the live-stock." Motioning toward the damage left by the fire, he added, "We'll have to postpone a honeymoon. It's impossible for us to go away now."

Dora nodded in agreement. "We'll start rebuilding tomorrow." She turned to Reverend Spencer. "Your voice is stronger than mine. Please tell everyone that I have insurance on the mill, and they can start moving the debris tomorrow to get ready for a new structure. Their wages will continue as usual."

Allen was among the first men to go into the wreckage of the building, and he was startled to see a body lying among the ashes—a body that had been struck down and pinned beneath a heavy log. Enough of the corpse remained so that it was easy to identify the body of Ted Morgan, which left no doubt that he was the one who'd started the fire. Although it seemed just punishment that he'd perished in the fire he had set to get even with Dora, Allen was still sorry for the man's misspent life. Morgan had had many good traits, but he'd been destroyed by his desire for revenge.

Dora had a considerable insurance policy on the property, and since most of the construction work was done by the mill workers, within three months Fairfield Textile Mill was operating again. Timothy took over management of the farm and lived there, while Allen and Dora stayed in the house she owned in Fairfield. Although she had family in

New York, the faithful Maude was willing to stay in North Carolina and keep house for them. Dora notified her father of their marriage, but he didn't respond to the letter.

Although her father's rejection hurt, Dora's heart overflowed with happiness, and Allen suggested that they should take their honeymoon. They asked one of their most capable and trustworthy employees to take over management of the mill for a week, so they could go away for a few days. When he asked Dora where she wanted to go, she said, "Why don't we go camping in the mountains? And take Kitty and Timothy with us. We've talked about such a trip for months. If we wait until we aren't busy— we never will go."

"It won't be much like a honeymoon if we take anyone with us, but the more I'm around my brother, the more impressed I am of how mature and capable he is. This will give you an opportunity to know him better. I hope he continues to stay with us."

Smiling, Dora answered, "I don't think he's going anywhere without Kitty, and I figure Mrs. Smith wouldn't approve of a wedding for another year or so."

Allen agreed that this was no doubt true, and a week later the four of them headed northwest. Their destination was a lovely camping spot in a secluded ravine near the Tennessee border. Although Kitty had lived all of her life in North Carolina, this was her first trip to this range of mountains. Allen had hunted in the area several autumns, and he knew enough about the area to guide them to the valley, where they set up camp. Allen and Timothy erected a tent for Dora and Kitty, but they preferred to sleep in the open.

On the first night, as soon as the sun eased slowly behind the mountains, they gathered around the campfire while Allen prepared their meal over the fire. He put whole potatoes in the hot ashes where they baked slowly. He had brought biscuits from home, and he turned T-bone steaks in the big skillet. Eating in the open was not a new experience for Dora because she and her father had often camped when they'd explored the mountains of Europe. However, she couldn't remember any time that those experiences had compared to this. She doubted that she would ever travel overseas again, although she would like to see more of the American continent.

As daylight faded and stars twinkled overhead, they were overwhelmed by the beauty of the universe.

"Tell us about the settlement of this area," Dora suggested to Allen.

Modestly, he answered, "I'm not the one to ask about that—you should discuss it with Vance the next time we visit them. But I'll tell you what I know."

Dora moved closer, and he put his arm around

her. Leaning against a large boulder, Allen said, "The Cherokee, of course, were well-established in these mountains before Europeans ever set foot on this continent, and that would have been sometime around the late 1600s. At first the native settlements were located in the river valleys. At the end of the French and Indian War, European settlers moved into this area. This caused a conflict with the Cherokee, who still held legal title to a great portion of the land. The Cherokee joined the British at the outbreak of the American Revolution, causing American forces to invade Cherokee Territory. Several years later the Cherokee were more or less forced to give control of the Great Smoky Mountains to the United States government.

"Although most of the natives moved westward along a road that was called the 'Trail of Tears,' other Cherokee hid in the mountains to escape forcible removal. They were the remnant who managed to keep their land and make up the eastern band of Cherokees in the Carolinas today."

"Why was it called the 'Trail of Tears'?" Dora asked.

"That was the name given when the government forced Native American nations from southeastern parts of the United States to move westward into what is now Oklahoma. They suffered from exposure, disease, and starvation before they reached their destination, and thousands of them died."

"Kinda sad, isn't it?" Timothy said.

Shrugging, Allen said, "That's what I've always thought, but if that hadn't happened, I wouldn't have the property I do today. I try not to criticize people of the past for what they've done, for who knows what decisions I would have made if I'd been in their shoes?"

Snuggling closer to him, Dora said, "I know what you would have done—you'd have made an honorable decision."

Allen put his arm around her waist. "You're prejudiced."

"That's true, but I'm looking forward to a long life with you and the people of North Carolina. Although I didn't know Him then, I realize now that God was guiding me when I decided to visit the Vanderbilts. I'm anticipating many happy years as your wife."

Epilogue

The next two years passed quickly as Allen and Dora adjusted slowly to marriage. They were both so self-reliant and independent that it was difficult for them to consider one another before they made decisions. However, as she contemplated the years they'd been together, Dora knew they had done well. They both brought to their union the determination that the marriage would work. As she thought of the months they'd been married, Dora knew they had slowly reached the realization that "two shall become one," as it was supposed to be.

The textile mill had prospered under their management. Fairfield had also increased in population—not so much that it had lost its small-town atmosphere, but enough that it was recognized as one of the most prosperous towns in western North Carolina.

From the first, Dora and Allen had planned to have children, and they were disappointed when two years passed before Dora finally became pregnant. Allen was surprised when she said one evening, a few weeks before their baby was due: "Would you mind if I turn the management of the mill over to you and become a full-time mother?"

Allen had hoped that Dora would come to this decision, but he'd been wise enough not to broach the subject. He'd always heard that pregnant women often developed cranky attitudes during their pregnancy, so he tried to be tactful in his response.

"Well, I don't know. It would be tough operating without you, but I can see why you would want to take care of the child yourself. I would be happier to know that you're taking care of our baby rather than some other woman."

Allen had always prided himself on being able to cope with any situation without undue concern, but as the day of the birth drew nearer, he was a nervous wreck. Six weeks before the child was to be born, Dora stopped going to the office. And despite the fact that Maude was with Dora, he went home every few hours to be sure she was all right.

Finally, Dora told him, "You're making me nervous. The doctor and Maude say that I'm doing great, so please stop fretting about me."

"You're nervous!" he said. "What about me? I can't keep my mind on anything except you and the baby."

Dora didn't have an easy delivery, and when the birth pains started, she tried to persuade Allen to go back to the office, but he refused and sat beside her hour after hour until the doctor finally told him it would be better for Dora if he would leave.

"She's in a lot of pain, which she tries to hide from you, and that will make the delivery more difficult. Why don't you take a walk? Or even sit on the porch and wait? If you want to help your wife, that's the best way to do it."

Unconvinced, Allen sat on the porch for several hours before Maude came out of the house, carrying a small bundle wrapped in a blanket.

"You've got a sweet little girl, Mr. Allen."

Allen jumped up quickly. "How's Dora?"

"She came through the delivery like a veteran. She's sleeping now."

Maude handed the baby to him. "Do you want to hold her?"

Being the oldest child in a large family of children, Allen was no amateur in caring for a child, so he took the baby eagerly. He sat down in a chair and rocked his baby for the first time. When the doctor came to the door and said Dora wanted to see him, he carried the baby into the bedroom and laid her beside his wife.

Kneeling beside the bed, he kissed her. "How are you?"

"Sleepy now. The doctor gave me some medicine, so the birth wasn't too bad. How do you like her?"

"She's wonderful—looks just like you must have looked when you were born."

She smiled slightly. "I don't remember that."

Although they'd discussed both boy and girl names, they couldn't agree on any definite choice. "What are we going to name her?" Allen asked.

"If it's all right with you, I'd like to give her my mother's name—Elizabeth Faye."

"Elizabeth Faye Bolden," Allen said. "I like it."

During their two years of marriage, Dora hadn't made any contact with her father, nor had he communicated with her. So she was surprised when she received a letter from him not long after Elizabeth's birth. Apparently he still subscribed to the Asheville newspaper and had read about the baby, or perhaps he had a spy in town who reported what she and Allen were doing. She wouldn't be at all surprised to learn he was doing that.

Daughter:
I know I haven't been a very good father.
Although I haven't contacted you the past few

years, I understand that you have prospered. I kept thinking you would make a failure of the mill and turn to me for help. That hasn't happened, so it's obvious you don't need my help. That makes me angry and happy at the same time. I'm happy because I have a daughter who's enough like me to make a success of anything you try. On the other hand, it's not flattering to not be needed. Regardless, I want you to know that I have written a new will that makes you my only heir, and there are no strings attached to it.

I'm so happy to know that you named the child for my beloved wife. If you and your husband can find it in your heart to forgive me for the past, I'd like to visit you sometime and see my granddaughter. Please let me know your reply.

Love,
Your Father

"What do you think I should do?" Dora asked Allen when she received the letter.

"I certainly don't want him to try to take control of Elizabeth's life, and I wonder if we can trust him."

"He may very well try to interfere in her life, but you and I have the upper hand in that situation. Having never known my own grandfather, I wouldn't want Elizabeth to be deprived of hers. I'd suggest that you make it very plain that the child is ours and that we'll not allow him to interfere. If he wants to act as a grandparent rather than a guardian, that will be all right."

"Will you answer the letter, please?"

In spite of what they suggested, Allen considered that Mr. Porter would still try to interfere in Elizabeth's life. He was determined that wouldn't happen, but he didn't want to offend the man. He prayed that God would give him the grace to handle the situation in a Christian manner. After a day of indecision, he sat at his office desk and spent an hour or two trying to compose a letter. He wasn't satisfied with his final draft, but he wrote the message, put it in an envelope, and took it to the post office.

> *Dear Mr. Porter:*
>
> *You're welcome to visit us at any time, but we believe it's only fair to tell you that we will not tolerate any interference from you as far as supporting the child is concerned. Our mill provides us with more than adequate income, and we can provide everything Elizabeth will ever need. What you do with your vast estate upon your death is your affair; however, we will not accept any large gifts of any kind for Elizabeth before she comes of age, when we will no longer have the right to accept or reject anything from you.*

If you're agreeable to the above stipulations, we will welcome you to our home at any time.

Sincerely,
Allen

Two weeks later when Mr. Porter arrived with boxes of gifts for the child and a repentant attitude, he was welcomed.

"I'm still very hazy on my Bible knowledge," Dora said, "but doesn't it say somewhere that, 'As ye would that men should do to you, do ye also to them likewise'?"

"Yes, and it might be one of the most important verses for us to know when we realize our responsibility not only to God, but also to others."

Although he stayed overnight at the local hotel, Mr. Porter spent most of his time at the house and, as far as they could tell, Dora and Allen believed that he wouldn't interfere with Elizabeth's upbringing.

After the birth of the baby and the reconciliation with Mr. Porter, Allen supposed their lives would settle down and they could continue without change for a few years. That didn't happen. Soon after Elizabeth's birth, Timothy came into the office one day, which wasn't unusual, but immediately Allen detected a difference in his brother.

"What's on your mind?" he asked.

Timothy took off his cap and twisted it in his hands. "Well, as you know," he started, "when I stopped here to see you, I was on my way to California."

Allen's stomach sank. When his brother hesitated, he prompted, "Yes?"

"I've liked it here, especially getting to know you and your family." He hesitated again. "But I've never given up the desire to cross the country to California. When I met Kitty and we loved each other, I thought I'd be happy here, but I'm not. It seems like there's something always over the next hill pulling me westward. Do you understand what I mean?"

Allen extended his hand across the desk, and Timothy grabbed it in a firm grip.

"I know exactly what you mean. It must be a family trait. That's why I left South Carolina years ago. I wasn't completely satisfied in Canaan, so I came here. I'll admit there have been times when I've looked westward and wondered what's over the next mountain, wondering if I'd stopped too soon."

Timothy smiled. "Then go with us."

Allen shook his head. "No. I made my choice when I married Dora. We have a good business here and she's happy. I wouldn't ask it of her, especially now that she has the baby."

"I'll bet she wouldn't hesitate one minute if you told her you wanted to go to California. She would say, 'When do we leave?' and start packing."

"I know that, but we can't do it now. It isn't only that we have Elizabeth, but what would we do with the textile mill? No doubt we could sell it, but we pamper our workers. A new owner might not be so generous and lenient as Dora is. You know that a transcontinental railroad already connects the East with California, and someday I intend for us to visit the West Coast, but not now. Do you plan to go on the railroad?"

With a sheepish grin, Timothy shook his head, pulled a sheet of paper from his pocket, and handed it to Allen. It was an ad from an Indiana paper, posted by a man who was organizing a wagon train trip from the Indianapolis area with San Francisco as his destination. "I've saved enough money to pay our fare."

"What does Kitty think about it?"

"Oh, she's as excited about it as I am, but her mother isn't."

Allen nodded. "That's understandable, but most parents have to deal with that. When will you leave?"

"I figure I'll have to go in two weeks to get to Indianapolis on time."

"Probably so. Well, I'm not going to discourage you or encourage you either. You're old enough to make decisions, but I'll help all I can. Choose the best wagon on the farm as well as a good team of horses. That will be your wedding present."

"Thanks. I've saved almost all the money you've

paid me for taking care of the farm, but I'll probably need all of that to buy supplies."

After Timothy left the office, Allen sat for a long time, envisioning the trip and the experiences, both good and bad. He knew if he mentioned to Dora that he'd always thought he would like to go to California, she would go with him without a murmur. However, he wouldn't ask it of her. So a month later, they stood with all the other Fairfield residents and watched Timothy and Kitty drive through town, westward bound.

Although Allen had tried to conceal his thoughts from Dora, he knew he hadn't succeeded. When the covered wagon passed out of sight and they turned toward their home, Dora said, "Never mind, my dear. As soon as they arrive at their destination and get settled, we'll go visit them. I've always dreamed of seeing California, but right now I've found all I want with you."

He lifted her hand and kissed the palm. "I know what you mean. God was looking after us when He brought both of us to Fairfield."

* * * * *

Author's Note

With the coming of the Western North Carolina Railroad in 1879, a new day dawned for Asheville, North Carolina. Because of the cool weather in the summer and a moderate winter climate, visitors were drawn to this plateau bordered by the Blue Ridge Mountains on the east and the Great Smoky Mountains on the west. Among the first settlers was George Vanderbilt, who first visited Asheville in 1888. Finding the air mild and invigorating, he enjoyed the scenery and soon made plans to build a summer residence in the area. Intending to replicate the working estates he'd visited in Europe, he commissioned a prominent New York architect to plan a house that featured ideas he'd learned from mansions he'd visited in the Loire Valley, France. He named the estate Biltmore, which included its own village. To make the property self-supporting, he established scientific forestry programs and separate farms for poultry, cattle, hogs, and also a dairy. After Vanderbilt's death in 1914, the estate was sold to the federal government.

ReaderService.com

Manage your account online!

- Review your order history
- Manage your payments
- Update your address

*We've designed
the Harlequin® Reader Service
website just for you.*

Enjoy all the features!

- Reader excerpts from any series
- Respond to mailings and special monthly offers
- Discover new series available to you
- Browse the Bonus Bucks catalog
- Share your feedback

Visit us at:

ReaderService.com

HEARTSONG PRESENTS

Look out for 4 new
Heartsong Presents books next month!

**Every month 4 inspiring faith-filled
romances will be available in stores.**

These contemporary and historical Christian
romances emphasize God's role in every
relationship and reinforce the importance of
faith, hope and love.

LIHP48648

Love Inspired®

To Trust or Not to Trust a Cowboy?

Former Dallas detective Jackson Stroud was set on moving to a new town for his dream job, until he makes a pit stop and discovers on the doorstep of a café an abandoned newborn and Shelby Grace, a waitress looking for a fresh start. He decides to help Shelby find the baby's mother, and through their quest he believes he's finally found a place to belong, while Shelby's convinced he will move on eventually. What will it take to convince Shelby that this is one cowboy she can count on?

Bundle of Joy
by
Annie Jones

Available March 2013!

www.LoveInspiredBooks.com

LI87801

Matchmaker—Matched!

For Ellie O'Brien, finding the perfect partner is easy—as long as
it's for the other people in the town of Peppin, Texas. When her
handsome childhood friend Lawson Williams jokingly proposes,
the town returns the favor and decides a romance is in order for
them. But when secrets in both their pasts threaten their future,
can the efforts of an entire town be enough to help them claim a
love as big and bold as Texas itself?

A TEXAS-MADE MATCH

by **Noelle Marchand**

Available in March wherever books are sold.

www.LoveInspiredBooks.com
LIH82957